HARLOT

The Asham Awards' third collection of stories

HARLOT RED

Prize-winning stories by women

Edited by Carole Buchan and Kate Pullinger

Library of Congress Catalog Card Number: 2001098873

A complete catalogue record for this book can be obtained from the British Library on request

The right of the individual contributors to be acknowledged as authors of their work has been asserted by them in accordance with the Copyright, Designs and Patents Act 1988

Copyright © 2002 of the individual contributions remains with the authors

Compilation Copyright © 2002 Carole Buchan and Kate Pullinger

First published in 2002
by Serpent's Tail,
4 Blackstock Mews, London N4 2BT
website: www.serpentstail.com

Set in Sabon by Intype London Ltd.
Printed in Great Britain by Mackays of Chatham plc

10 9 8 7 6 5 4 3 2 1

Contents

❦

Foreword

If you think all those hundreds of unknown women scribbling away on the kitchen table are penning the next Aga-saga, then think again. This anthology of stories from the winners of the third Asham Award is no cosy collection of writing about safe, comfortable domesticity.

This year's writers explore the whole range of human experience – sad, funny, often uncomfortable, sometimes frightening. There is disappointment, lust, betrayal, and there is warmth and friendship too. These are stories which have freshness and spontaneity, by writers not afraid to push beyond the conventional boundaries.

Our thanks to the already well-known writers who have contributed to this collection and whose stories appear alongside those of the winners. We very much value the support and enthusiasm shown over the years by these writers who provide such an inspiration for the hundreds of women who enter this biennial competition. Special thanks also to our chair of judges, novelist Kate Pullinger, who has edited the anthology and who gave so much help and advice to the winning writers.

Nearly 1,000 women entered this third competition. We hope you share our enthusiasm for the judges' choices and agree that with *Harlot Red*, the Asham Award has come of age.

Carole Buchan
Asham Literary Endowment Trust
Lewes, East Sussex

Asham Awards 2002

First prize   Frances Childs
Second prize   Jenny Mitchell
Joint third prize Tania Casselle and
                     Rowena Macdonald

Here's

Carol Shields

It's the year 2000, the first year of the twenty-first century, and here's what I've written so far in my life. Or rather, what has been officially published (I'm not including my old schoolgirl sonnets from the seventies: *Satin slippered April, you glide through time/ And lubricate spring days, de dum, de dum*, and my dozen or so book reviews). So here's my writing life, as of today:

1. A translation and Introduction to/of Danielle Westerman's book of poetry, *Isolation*, April, 1981, one month before our daughter Norah was born, a home birth naturally; a midwife; you could almost hear the guitars plinking in the background, though we did not feast on the placenta as some of our friends were doing at the time. Naturally, I'm a little uneasy about posting *Isolation* as my own writing, but Dr Westerman, doing one of her hurrying, over-the-head gestures, insists that translation, especially poetry, is a creative act. Writing and translating are convivial, she says, not oppositional, and certainly not hierarchical. My '*Introduction*' to *Isolation*, though, was definitely creative, for it seems I had no idea what I was talking about.

I hauled it out of the file and read it recently, and experienced the Burrowing of the Palpable Worm of Shame, as a friend of mine calls it. Such pretension; it's hilarious, actually. The part about art transmuting the despair of life to the 'merely frangible', and poetry's attempt to 'repair the gap between ought and naught' – what on earth did I mean? Too much Derrida and friends might be the problem. I was into all that pretty heavily in the early eighties.

2. Next: 'The Brightness of a Star', a short story that appeared in *An Anthology of Young Ontario Voices* published by the Pink Onion Press, 1985. It's hard to believe that I qualified as 'a young voice' in 1985 but, in fact, I was only twenty-seven, mother of Norah, aged four, her sister Christine, aged two, and about to give birth to Nancy – in a hospital this time. Three daughters, and not even thirty. 'How did you find the time?' people used to chorus, and in that query I often registered an intimation of blame: was I neglecting my darling sprogs for my writing career? Well, no. I never thought in terms of career. I *dabbled* in writing. It was my macramé, my knitting, but not long after that I started to get serious and joined a local 'writers' workshop for women, which met once a week, for two hours, at the Y where we drank coffee and had a good time, feeling privileged to be in each other's company, and that led to:

3. 'Icon', a short story, 1986. Gwen Reidman, a writer, the only published author in the workshop group, was our leader. The Glenmar Collective (an acronym of our first names – not very original) was what we called ourselves. Gwen said, moving a muffin to her mouth, that she was moved by the 'austerity' of my one completed short story – which was based, but only roughly, on my response to the Russian Icon show at the Ontario Art Gallery. My fictional piece was a case of art 'embracing/repudiating art', as Gwen put it, and then she reminded us of the famous 'On First Looking

into Chapman's Homer', and the whole aesthetic of art begetting art, which I no longer believe in, by the way. Either you do or you don't. The seven of us, Gwen, Lorna, Emma, Nan, Marcella, Annette, and I (My name is Reta Winters), self-published our pieces – one each – in a volume titled *Incursions and Interruptions*, and all we had to do was throw in $50 each for the printing bill. The 800 copies sold quickly in the local bookstores, mostly to our friends and family members. Publishing was cheap, it turned out. What a surprise. We called ourselves The Stepping Stone Press, and in that name we expressed, I think, our mild embarrassment at the idea of self-publishing, but also the hope that we would 'step' up to authentic publishing eventually. (Gwen, of course, was already there.)

4. *Alive (Pour Vivre)*, 1987, Random House, a translation of Volume One of Danielle Westerman's memoirs. Again I seem to be claiming translation as an act of originality, but (and again) Danielle, in her benign way, wrinkling her disorderly forehead, has urged me to think that the act of shuffling elegant French into readable and stable English is an aesthetic performance. The book did very well in terms of critical response, and even sold moderately well, a dense but popular book, offered without shame and nary a footnote. The translation itself was slammed in the *Toronto Star* ('clumsy') by one Stanley Harold Hogarth, but Danielle Westerman said never mind: the man is *un maquereau*, which translates, crudely, into something between a pimp and a prick. A cad, people might have said forty years ago.

5. I then wrote a commissioned pamphlet for a series of such pamphlets put out by a press calling itself Encyclopédie de L'Art. The press produced tiny, hold-in-the-hand booklets, each devoted to a single subject,

covering everything from Braque to Calder to Klee to Mondrian to Villon. The editor in New York (operating out of a phone booth, it seems and knowing nothing of my ignorance) had stumbled on my short story 'Icon', and believed me to be an expert on the subject. He asked for 3,000 words for a volume (volumette, really) to be called *Russian Icons*, published finally in 1989. It took me a whole year to do this, what with Tom and the three girls, and the house and garden and meals and laundry and too much inwardness. They published my 'text', such a crisp cold-water word, along with a series of coloured plates, in both English and French (I did the French as well) and paid me $400. I learned all about the schools of Suzdal and Vladimir and what went on in Novgorod (a lot) and how images of saints made medieval people tremble with fear. The book was never reviewed to my knowledge, but I can read it today without shame. It is almost impossible to be pseudo when writing about paintings that know no rules of perspective, and that are done on slabs of ordinary wood.

6. I lost a year or two after this, which I don't understand, since all three girls had started school, though Nancy was only in morning kindergarten. I think I was too busy thinking about the business of *being* a writer, about being writerly and fretting over Tom's ego and needing my own writing space and turning thirty and feeling older than I've ever felt since; my age – thirty – stared at me all the time, standing tall and wide-shouldered in my head, and blocking access to what my life afforded. All this anguish was unnecessary. Tom's ego was unchallenged by my slender publications. He was not driven twenty-four hours a day to rescue himself from insignificance. We put a skylight in the box room,

bought a used office desk, and I sat down and translated Danielle Westerman's immense *Les Femmes et le Pouvoir*, published in 1992. In English the title was changed to *Women Waiting*, which only makes sense if you've read the book (Women possess power, but it is power that has yet to be seized, ignited and released and so forth). This time no one grumped about my translation. 'Sparkling and full of ease,' the *Globe* said, and the *New York Times* went one better and called it 'an achievement'.

'You are my true sister,' said Danielle Westerman at the time. *Ma vrai soeur.* I hugged her back; she has a craving for physical touch, which has not slackened in her eighties, though nowadays it is mostly her physician who touches her or the manicurist (she is the only person I know who has her nails done twice a week, beautiful long nailbeds, matching her long quizzing eyes).

7. I was giddy. All at once there were translation offers arriving in the mail, but I kept thinking I could maybe write short stories, even though our Glenmar group was dwindling, with Emma getting a job, Annette being hit with a divorce, and Gwen moving to the States. The trouble was I hated my short stories. Fiction sent me into whimsy mode, and although I believed whimsicality to be a strand of the human personality, I was embarrassed at what I was pumping into my new Apple computer, sitting there under the pure brightness of the skylight. Pernicious, precious. I was so awfully fetching with my 'Ellen was setting the table and she knew tonight would be different'. A little bug sat in my ear and muttered: Who cares about Ellen and her woven placemats and her hopes for the future?

I certainly didn't care.

Because of having three kids, everyone said I should

be writing kiddy lit, But I couldn't find the voice. It screeched in my throat. Talking ducks and chuckling frogs. I wanted something sterner and more finite as a task, which is how I came to write: *Shakespeare and Flowers*, Cyclone Press, San Francisco, 1994. The contract was negotiated before I wrote one word. Along came a little bundle of cash to start me off and the rest promised on publication. A scholarly endeavour, I thought, but I ended up with a wee 'giftie' book. You could send this book to anyone on your list who was maidenly or semi-academic or who you didn't know very well. At sixty-eight pages it would fit into a small mailer.

Shakespeare and Flowers was sold in the kind of outlets that stock greeting cards and stuffed bears. I simply scanned the Shakespeare canon and picked up references to, say, the eglantine (*Midsummer Night's Dream*) or the blackberry (*As You like It*) and then I puffed out a little description of the flower, and conferenced on the phone (twice) with the illustrator in Berkeley, and used lots of quotes. A sweet little book, excellent slick paper, $12.95 US. It sold two hundred thousand copies, and is still selling. They'd like me to do something on Shakespeare and animals, and I just might.

8. *Eros: Essays*, by Danielle Westerman, translation by Reta Winters. Hugely successful, despite a tiny advance. Tom and I and the girls took the first translation payment and went to France for a month, southern Burgundy, a village called La Roche-Vineuse, where Danielle had grown up, halfway between Cluny and Macon, red-tiled roofs set in the midst of rolling vineyards. Our rental house was built around a cobbled courtyard full of ancient roses and hydrangeas. 'How

old is this house,' we asked the neighbours, who invited us in for an *apéritif*. 'Very old,' was all we got. The stone walls were two feet thick. The girls took tennis lessons at *l'ecole d'été*, and Tom went hacking for trilobites and I sat in a wicker chair in the flower-filled courtyard, reading novels day after day, and thinking: I want to write a novel. That is what I really want to do.

I didn't think about our girls growing older and leaving home and falling into tragedy. Norah had been a good, docile baby and then she became a good obedient little girl, and now, at age nineteen, she's so brimming with goodness that she sits on a Toronto street corner with a begging bowl and asks nothing of the world. Nine-tenths of what she gathers she distributes at the end of the day to other street people. She embodies goodness, or at least she is on the path – so she said in our last conversation, which was twelve weeks ago, April 3rd. Her long, pale hair was matted. She refused to look us in the eye, but she did blink – I'm sure of it – when I handed her a sack of cheese sandwiches and Tom dropped a roll of twenty-dollar bills in her lap. Then she spoke, in her own voice, but a voice emptied of connection. She could not come home. She was on the path to goodness. She could not be diverted. She could not 'be' with us.

We don't know how this happened, but we know it didn't rise out of the ordinary plot lines of a life story. An intelligent and beautiful girl from a loving family grows up in Orangetown, Ontario, her mother's a writer, her father's a doctor, the two younger sibs are funny and smart, and then she goes off the track. There's nothing natural about this efflorescence of goodness. It's abrupt and brutal. It's killing us. (What will really kill us, though, is the day we *don't* find her sitting on her square of pavement.)

But I didn't know any of this when I sat in that Burgundy garden dreaming about writing a novel. I thought I understood something of a novel's architecture, the lovely slope of predicament, the tendrils of surface detail, the calculated curving upward into inevitability, and then the ending, a complicity of cause and effect and the gathering together of all the characters into a framed circle of consolation and ecstasy, backlit with fibre-optic gold, just for a moment, just for a second.

I had an idea for my novel. I had two appealing characters, a woman and a man, Alicia and Roman.

9. And I had a title, *My Thyme is Up*. It was a pun, of course. It came from an old family joke, and I meant to write a jokey novel. A light novel. A novel for summertime, a book to read while seated in an Ikea wicker chair with the sun falling on the pages as lightly and evenly as through a Japanese lattice. Naturally it would have a happy ending. I never doubted but that I could write this novel, and I did (1998).

10. *The Middle Years*, the translation of Volume Three of Danielle Westerman's memoirs. It's coming out this fall, in late September. Volume Three explores Westerman's numerous love affairs with both men and women, and none of this will be shocking or even surprising to her readers. What will be new is the suppleness and strength of her sentences. Always an artist of concision and selflessness, she has arrived in her old age at a gorgeous fluidity and expansion of phrase. My translation doesn't begin to express what she has accomplished. It's stark; it's also sentimental; one balances and rescues the other, oddly enough. It's as

though those endless calcium pills Danielle tosses down every morning and the vitamin E and the emu oil capsules have streamed directly into her vein of language, so that what lands on the page is larger, more rapturous, more self-forgetful than anything she's written before, and all of it sprouting with short, swift digressions that pretend to be just careless asides, little swoons of surrender to her own experience, inviting us, her readers, to believe in the totality of her abandonment.

Either that or she's gone senile to good effect. The thought has more than once occurred to me.

Another thought has drifted by, silken as a breeze that goes unrecorded. There's something missing in these memoirs, I think, in my solipsistic view. Danielle Westerman suffers, she feels the pangs of existential loneliness, the absence of sexual love, the treason of her own body. But she doesn't have a lost child, and perhaps it's this that makes the memoirs themselves childlike. They go down like good milk, foaming, swirling in the glass.

11. I shouldn't mention Book Number Eleven since it is not a *fait accompli*, but I will. I'm going to write a second novel, a sequel to *My Thyme is Up*. I have no idea what will happen in this book. It is a mere abstraction at the moment, something that's popped out of the ground like the hard, rounded shoot of a crocus on a cold lawn. I've stumbled up against it in my clumsy manner, and now the feeling of it won't go away. It's going to be about lost children, about goodness, and going home and being happy at home and trying to stay alive off the poison of the printed page. I'm desperate to know how it's going to turn out.

Harlot Red

Magi Gibson

The carriage rocks and sways, hurtles her through sun-drenched countryside. Fields, golden as childhood rush towards her, then past. She tips her head back against the seat and closes her eyes on the sky's naked stare. Flecks of red and black explode behind her closed lids.

She stands again by the harbour wall. When she first left she had planned never to return. A gentle breeze lifts a stray strand of hair and she pushes it back from her eyes, tucks it firmly behind one ear. The bay curves in a perfect horseshoe and on the far side she can see the row of whitewashed fishermen's cottages, their windows shimmering in the morning sun. She can make out the black ribbon of road and his car parked there, as though it had never moved in the six months she had been gone. Squinting against the sun, she lets her eyes run over the black volcanic rocks, the pebbled beach, the dark ribbon of seaweed and flotsam left by the night's high tide, the froth of waves teasing the damp sand.

She pulls her coat tighter. Late September this far north the wind is bitter. It finds its way through the thin material of her city clothes and its icy fingers nip and pinch her skin. She lifts one hand and shields her eyes against the glistening sea. Her brain counts along the painted doors of the cottages at the far side of the bay and stops five along, at the red door. *Post box red* she had said when they first moved in. *Harlot red* he had said. *Harlot red for the scarlet woman who shares my bed.* The door shimmers in the thin air, as if not a real door at all. But she knows it is old and solid and wooden. She wonders if he is perhaps behind it, maybe shuffling sleepily from the front bedroom where he sleeps (where once she slept) to the kitchen, thinking about coffee.

But it's not yet eight o'clock. He might still be in bed. When she was there they would wake about seven. They'd lie, tangled together, then they'd fuck. She liked fucking in the morning. *Better than black coffee.* That's what she always said to him. *Best way in the world to wake up.* She thinks of his fingers exploring her skin, but then a new thought, a fear, hits her like a bullet: she has not spoken to him for over six months, he might not be

alone

her mind jumps

jolts

a hundred volts

fired through it

and then, like in a flickering home movie, she sees

the dishevelled bed, the white cotton sheets, the patchwork quilt, rich in golds and browns, like fallen autumn leaves, and him tangled in it, one leg stretched languid from the covers, tanned against the white cotton

alone

one arm dragged lazily above his head, the dark patch of hair in his underarm

and he turns

—[11]—

and a seagull shrieks above her, the sharpness of its call snipping the spinning reel of film and the image of him cuts, whirrs into blackness.

But her mind slips back to his room again. And though she knows she is standing by the harbour wall, and though she feels the cold wind's fingers nip her skin, she remembers the smell of his body, damp and musky after sleep and deep between her hips she . . .

'Good morning, Jenni! A while since we've seen you.' She spins around, startled at the sudden intrusion, startled at the sound of her own name. Young Rab, the postman, waves cheerily from the other side of the road. She waves back, shivers and blinks as she sees

the red door on the far side of the bay open.

He does not know, cannot know that she has returned, she thinks as she watches him leave the cottage, his dark coat buttoned against the breeze, his yellow scarf flapping soft arms at her.

He pulls the red door shut and she watches him stride along to the corner then turn up the steep hill that leads to the station. She closes her eyes and breathes in deep the salt air, lets it fill her lungs, push out the city grime that has silted them these last few months.

He will be at the station now, she figures as she starts to walk briskly around the bay, relieved that at last she is moving and the blood is warming in her veins. She blows on her cupped hands. A cup of coffee, strong and black, would be good right now, she thinks.

She walks briskly along the beach, leaving a trail of footprints in the damp sand. Small waves rush towards her like over-eager pups. She feels her heart race with them and curses her own over-eagerness. He will be on the station platform now, the morning paper tucked under his arm. He will be watching for the train snaking its way from Aberdeen, the train she'd come back on this morning while he slept. It will grind to a halt and he will board it. And then he will be gone to work all day in the city.

She stops and gazes out across the waves. Her eyes scan the horizon, struggle to make out the thin line where sea and sky meet. But they merge in a oneness. It is impossible to say where one finishes and the other begins. She bends and picks a dappled pebble from the beach. Thousands of years being rolled and washed by the ocean has left it round and smooth. She puts it to her lips and tastes the salt coldness, then slips it in her pocket.

As she turns to walk towards the cottage she sees Young Rab watching her. When she first moved to the village he was a gangly twelve-year-old, falling over himself to run errands for her, to please her. *That boy's got a crush on you*, he had said and she'd wondered at the jealous edge in his voice. At the time it had seemed so ridiculous. But Rab is no longer a gangly twelve-year-old. He is a young man now, a young man with broad shoulders and a shy smile.

Close up the cottage seems much the same. She allows herself a little laugh, allows a smile to curl the corners of her mouth. What had she been expecting? Its white-washed stone and cold grey slate had been there for a hundred years before they had bought it. Its walls had silently held the pain of births and deaths. Of course the cottage has remained the same. Yet, she thinks, she has changed so much, has grown so much.

The closer she comes to it, the more wary she feels, as if she is treading on the graves of the dead. A swarm of *what ifs* begin buzzing in her head like startled bees:

what if he has found someone else? What if she peers in the window and sees a woman sitting at the kitchen table, tousle-haired, hands clasped around a mug? She hadn't left him a contact address, hadn't left him a number. She had intended cutting him right out of her life. It had seemed important at the time. It had been a matter of survival. She was merging with him, becoming subsumed by him. She'd needed to re-establish her own identity, she'd needed her independence. *I'll contact you if I need anything,* she'd said. *Anything I've left behind.*

As if a hand has snatched at her coat, holding her back, she stops. Behind her the sea rushes and sucks, a few seagulls strut the wet sands, others swoop over the waves, calling. She glances along the empty street. They'd lain together in bed a thousand times, him peppering her breasts and belly with playful kisses, and joked about this tiny place, this ghost town they'd come to. *There'll be tumbleweed rolling along the street in the morning* he'd whispered once. *We'll wake and discover we're the only people left in the world. Adam and Eve.*

She turns and walks up to the shining red door. The scarlet door. Perhaps she should ring the bell? Perhaps he has found himself a new Eve and she now lay drowsed in his bed. Perhaps the new woman (whom he had sworn he would never find, because there could be no other woman for him), perhaps the new woman will be startled by her sudden arrival.

She presses the bell and listens as its chime dances around the shadows then fades. She presses again and again until the notes collide into each other in a wild cacophony, then merge into silence. And when no tousle-haired woman answers, she slips her key in the lock, pushes the door open, steps into the silence.

The mirror edged with shells she once gathered from

the beach stares at her accusingly. She turns her head away. She shouldn't be doing this, shouldn't be creeping like a burglar into his home. She had chosen to leave. She had told him she no longer needed him and had chosen to leave and go. *You'll soon come back*, he had said. And she had cursed his cockiness, his arrogance. *You're the kind of woman who needs a man.*

She glances around the kitchen. It is tidier than she remembered. The plates are neatly stacked on the shelf, matching mugs hang smugly from new hooks. His walking boots lie by the back door, cleaned and polished. She kneels down beside them and strokes their smooth leather. His dark green cagoule brushes her cheek. She thinks of him coming in from walks by the winter sea, his cheeks damp from the salt spray, his hair wild and curling where the wind's salt fingers have teased it. He liked to go out early in the morning when she was drowsy. He'd come back his cheeks tinged pink, his hands cold, and she would stand naked against him and nuzzle his neck and lick the salt from his face.

She takes her coat off and hangs it on the hook beside his cagoule. It pleases her to think of these garments hanging tangled together like lovers. She slips her shoes off, arranges them neatly beside his boots, then walks barefoot through to his bedroom.

He must have made the bed quickly, she thinks, as she throws the quilt back and gazes at the faint imprint of his body on the sheet. She stands for a moment at the small window looking out across the bay, then pulls down the blind. The room softens to a tawny glow in the filtered light. She turns the chevalier mirror towards the bed, slightly angles it, so she will be able to watch herself.

She stands before the mirror. Her soft jumper curves

demurely over her breasts. Underneath she is wearing black. *I like you best in lace* he'd murmured once, then he'd pushed the cups of her bra down with his thumbs until her nipples, rosy as twin early morning suns, had risen from the darkness. He'd kissed each one until she'd felt them rise beneath his tongue like perfect stalks on perfect apples.

The mirror watches as she pulls the jumper slowly up over her head. She pushes the lace of her bra down and her nipples peek out. For a moment she stands like that, then slides her hands over the slight swell of her stomach, waits for his footfall in the hall, for the door to swing open and him to be standing there, wanting her.

She unzips her jeans, the purr of the descending zip loud in the silence of the room. She smiles at her reflection as she imagines him in the bed waiting for her, watching her.

Slowly, she wanders through to the living room, aware that here she can be seen from the road. Maybe young Rab the Postie will pass by, she muses as she flicks through his CDs. Maybe young Rab will press his face against the window and watch. She takes Tom Waits from the rack, slides him into the machine, turns him low, lets his voice stroke her skin with its cat-tongue roughness. She crosses to the window and looks out, but young Rab is nowhere to be seen. Shame, she thinks. Last summer she'd seen him swimming in the sea. She unclips her bra and sets her breasts free. Maybe she should seek him out before she goes back tonight, ask him to call in on her if he's ever in the city.

Tom Waits is moaning low, his voice mixing in with the ocean's purr. Back in the bedroom she pushes the jeans slowly down, down over her thighs, kicks them to the floor. Then she angles the mirror a little deeper, enters the empty bed.

She closes her eyes while her fingers explore the damp velvet softness. She thinks of a deep red rose, its petals folded dew-laden and silken around the small hard centre of its sweetness.

Then she thinks of him, in his office, at his desk. Talking on the phone to a client. Her fingers dig deeper.

She opens her eyes and smiles at the rise of her breasts. Her fingers are busy still, expertly stroking and caressing. Sex had been good with him. That was what she misses most. Her breathing becomes shallower, sharper. She misses his tongue, his fingers. She imagines him at his desk again, her head in his lap, her fingers undoing his zip . . . her hips rock rhythmically in time with the suck and rush of the ocean. The orgasm shudders through her belly in rippling waves . . . for a moment

the world does not
exist.

She leaves the pebble she had picked from the beach, smooth and rounded by the waves, in his bed. A dappled pebble, freckled like his skin. A pebble she'd held in her mouth, held in her fingers, held in the soft folds of her skin.

She stands on the platform at the station, the sky streaked now with clouds floating in wisps low and fast across the blue. The sun is warmer away from the cold sea wind and she can feel sweat prickle her skin beneath the soft jumper.

You can't be serious, he'd said when she packed her bags, sat them at the door, told him her mind was made up. *You'll be back in a fortnight*, he'd said. *You'll not be happy on your own. Who's going to look after the bills? Who's going to fix the heating if it breaks down? Who's going to get up in the middle of the night when you hear a strange noise? You're fooling yourself. You need me.*

She glances at her watch then lifts her eyes and lets them follow the line of the shining metal tracks. They curve and converge, two tracks into one, then split again and go their separate ways.

At last she sees the train snake towards her, through the sunlight, through the fields and bushes. In a few more hours he will alight from it, his dark coat unbuttoned, his scarf tucked in his pocket.

He will find the pebble when he goes to bed tonight, when he puts the lamp out and slips naked between the cool sheets. It will dig into the muscle of his thigh and his fingers will pull it from where it has been resting. He will switch the lamp back on and a bemused look will flit across his face. Then, maybe, he'll smell her, the faint trace of her perfume in the air, or maybe then he'll notice a few long hairs on his pillow, a smudge of lipstick. Maybe the waves and wind will whisper her name.

She will think of this, while she sits in her city flat, her cheek against the cold glass, as she stares out at the trail of tail lights fizzing red in the September drizzle, at the dark windows, at the people scurrying home.

And maybe behind the harlot red door, he'll stroke the pebble, stroke it as once he stroked her, or place it to his lips and taste its salt with his tongue.

And maybe he'll realise then what she really needed him for.

Prospect House

Frances Childs

When I first arrived at Prospect House the other girls stared at me with a mixture of wary contempt and vague interest. I'd come from London you see, the city. I might think I was harder than them, might want to throw my weight around. Not that I had much weight, I was as thin as a rake, yellow and emaciated, recovering from a bad dose of Hep B.

I'd caught Hep B off a bloke whose name I couldn't now remember. I'd sneaked him into the bedroom I shared with Anna and fucked him all night. Anna was outraged, hugely high on moral indignation. She enjoyed it I think, being angry with me. Anyway the bloke was nice looking and I enjoyed myself. But I did suffer for my sins, did pay my penance. I caught a nasty venereal disease and got booted out of the home for deprived children where Anna and I were working.

It makes me smile now, when I think about it. Makes me giggle to myself that I was working in that northern seaside town in a holiday home for deprived children when I was little more than a child myself. Anyway, there I was out on my ear after my sex romp with the bloke with the pierced nipple. All the other people working in the home sided with Anna, thought I'd behaved despicably, so I collected my week's wages and hitched to London.

After a while I ended up at Prospect House, a home for single teenage girls. Most of them weren't there all that long, they got pregnant pretty quick and were shipped out to the mother and baby unit up the road. I went to visit Gina there with her baby Chantelle. All I could hear were the screams of these babies, born to girls who wanted someone to love them. Sometimes I heard the girls screaming as well as their babies. Screaming in anger, rage, frustration. It was a horrible ragged primitive sound, the screams of these teenage mothers. Girls who'd never had a mother themselves, didn't know how to do it, hadn't learnt the ropes.

Gina was a plump ginger girl with freckles. She came out of care and went into Prospect House. She cleaned up at the local hospital for a bit and then she got pregnant and moved into the mother and baby unit at Sussex House. At least they didn't bother calling it Hope House, or New Initiative Place; at least by that time, by the time the girls were transferred to Sussex House, they'd stopped pretending.

By the time I went to see Gina and Chantelle at their dirty damp institution with its peeling plaster walls and its smell of boiled cabbage, I wasn't yellow anymore. My illness had made the Prospect girls frightened of me, I'd thrown a knife at Di, not to really hurt her, more to see if I could get away with it and I had. She'd sworn at me but not punched me.

'You slag, what the fuck are you doing?'

I picked the knife up, a long sharp bread knife, 'Nothing,' I said and smiled at her. Andrea looked at me out of her hooded eyes; she was enormously fat. I thought she might haul herself out of her chair and lump me one but she didn't. Di went and sat next to her; they both looked at me as I walked slowly out of the room.

Once I wasn't yellow anymore, though, I lost some of my mystique and then Andrea and Di gave me a good hiding. Di, who was about eleven stone, sat on me whilst fifteen-stone Andrea punched me mechanically around the head. I didn't really mind. After that, some of the tension in the house disappeared and we were all able to get along quite well.

I saw an advert in the paper for a local Am Dram group; they were performing a play, *The Crucible*. I'd always fancied having a go at acting.

Andrea comes home from the chicken-plucking job that our annoying project worker has made her get.

'I fucking hate that fucking place,' she says as she collapses into a chair and unwraps a chicken pie she's brought from the chippie on the way home.

'What do you have to do?' I ask. 'Do you have to kill the chickens as well?' I can imagine her killing chickens, wringing their necks with her podgy white hands.

'Course not,' she says with her mouth full. I can see bits of grey stuff swilling around inside her pink mouth. 'That's the blokes that do that. I just pull their feathers out. It's fucking boring.'

'Never mind,' says Di, who likes to make people feel better. 'You won't have to do it for long.'

'Yeah, just until that slag Linda gets off my back.'

Linda is a large, matronly middle-aged lady who is our project worker and comes round in the morning and shouts at us to get out of bed. We like her really, she's kind to us and she reminds us of the mothers we might have had. I don't think we'd be very happy if she didn't bother to tell us off. Di and Andrea have aunties, women who worked in the care homes they were in. They talk about these aunties often. Auntie Sue, Auntie Liz, Auntie Ann, but I've never met any of them. I've never met a single auntie.

'Kim wants to go into one of them shows,' Di says helping herself to a chip.

'Do you?' Andrea looks at me. 'What shows?'

'In the paper,' I say, 'they're advertising for people to act in a play.'

Andrea smiles at me, her green eyes, which are very beautiful even though they are half hidden, squashed up beneath her flesh, smile at me. 'You'd be good in a play,' she says.

'Wouldn't she, Di?'

'Yeah,' Di nods her peroxide head vigorously, 'that's what I said.'

Gentle buxom blue-eyed Di starts seeing Rob, one of the local boys. He comes to the house often. When he's not there we laugh at him. Andrea has slept with him as well and she and Di laugh at the size of his cock, which they say is tiny. He's quite hard so we wouldn't dare laugh at him to his face, but when he's gone either Di or Andrea will hold up their thumb and forefinger, about two centimetres apart and we will laugh.

'Why are you sleeping with him then?' I ask one day.

Di shrugs. 'Better than nothing, isn't it?'

Andrea cackles. 'Is it? I couldn't feel nothing, I thought he'd finished and he hadn't, he was still at it. Pumping up and down like a dick head.' They laugh. I suspect Di is trying to get pregnant.

'Don't get pregnant, Di,' I say. 'You'll end up at Sussex House.'

'It's not forever though, is it?' she says. 'You get your own flat in the end.'

'Gina's had her kid taken off her.' Di opens a packet of Mr Kipling jam tarts and passes them round. 'Social took her kid away.'

'Did they?' Andrea's not very interested.

'Yeah, she was hitting the kid or something, had to take it to hospital.'

'I've got my audition tomorrow,' I say.

'Do you want us to come with you?' Andrea offers.

'No thanks,' I say.

That night I hear a commotion in the bathroom upstairs. I had been asleep and the scuffles and whimpers took some time to wake me. I thought that they were part of my dream, a nagging interference. When I do wake up I am momentarily disoriented, lie in my bed in the pitch-black room trying to collect my thoughts. A scream has me up like a shot. I put the light on. I can hear Di crying and shouting. I get a thick wooden coat hanger out of the cupboard and run up the stairs. The bathroom door is open. I can see Di half naked, Rob shoving at her and behind him Andrea yanking his hair. He's trying to elbow Andrea away from him. I pass her the coat hanger. There isn't room for me in the bathroom as well. She whacks him over the head with it.

He screams in pain and rage and stumbles out down the stairs and into the night. We have a cup of tea and a fag together.

'Don't let that bastard back in the house,' says Andrea.

'I won't.' Di is looking all right although she's got the beginnings of a black eye. 'He was beating me up because he said I was flirting with Danny. I won't let him back in the house,' she says. We know she will. He's better than nothing, after all.

'You'd better go to bed, Kim.' Di pats me on the head, you've got your thing tomorrow.'

'Audition,' I say.

'Do you remember when Kim first moved in?' Andrea lights another fag. 'We thought you was a right stuck-up cunt.'

'Yeah, you was all yellow and you wouldn't speak to no one.'

'I was shy,' I say.

'Shy, my arse.' Andrea lets out a fart to emphasise her point. 'You was just stuck up.'

The next morning, the police come round at about six and nick Andrea; someone has tipped them off. Her room is full of stolen electrical equipment that some boys she knows from care were storing with her.

'What'll happen to her?' I ask Di who is still in bed. She's waiting 'til Linda comes round before she gets up.

'Dunno,' she scratches her blonde curls, 'not much, she won't be in much trouble, magistrates are soft on Prospect girls. At least she won't have to work at that shit job no more.'

'Why not?'

'Kim!' Di shouts. 'Get out, you slag, it's only nine o'clock, get out and stop asking all them questions.'

I wander off to the audition. It's not like I'd expected. It's in a room with a lot of other people. They are all sitting around in a circle. A man in a purple velvet shirt gives me some papers.

'Welcome, welcome,' he says. 'Sit yourself down and please enter your name and address on the rather official-looking form that's wending its way around the room.' I want to giggle but know that this would be a bad idea. I try and smile at Mr Twat and then find a seat. I'm next to a lady with long grey hair swept up into a bun. She's wearing bright orange lipstick. 'Hello,' she says. I notice some of her lipstick has come off onto her teeth.

The form arrives. I scribble my name and address down and pass it on. Most people here are much older than me. I feel a bit comforted, I'd have been very nervous if they'd all been my age, but older people are gentler, kinder, won't take the piss if I stumble over the words. I suppose it'll be like at school in English literature classes when we had to read out loud. God, what a torture listening to all those monotones mispronouncing words, heaving and sighing before each speech. I start reading the bits of paper I've been given. I want Abigail, that's the only part I want. I'm desperate for it. As I read I realise I've never wanted anything so much in my life. I want to be that scarlet woman, that Jezebel, that beautiful bitch. I want to let myself go, to hyperventilate, to point the accusing finger. I start to imagine myself in that bare courtroom, with its sanded wooden floor, its simple cross, suffering crucified Christ gazing down at us, at all of us, his lost lambs, the lost souls he died for that we might be saved. I see myself in my long black dress, my simple white bonnet framing my young virginal creamy face. I see myself centre stage screaming as the demons rise before me, as Lucifer, lonely angry Lucifer beckons me to him, begs me to have mercy, that he should not be forever cast out, banished from the possibility of redemption.

A voice cuts across my thoughts, a shrill female voice. It comes from one of the middle-aged ladies in the corner. A sharp bob haircut, smart black trouser suit, at her neck a string of pearls.

'Oh, look at this,' she says. 'We've got a Prospect House girl here.' She laughs. Some other people chortle with her. It's all good-natured, gentle fun. I smile, self-deprecatingly. I smile and lower my head. 'You bitch,' I think. 'You fucking bitch. I'll get that part now if it fucking kills me.'

As I read I know that I am Abigail. I know I am that girl, motherless, seething with desire, pushed into a world that cannot accommodate her. I know that I am her, she who makes her own magic, she who will have what she wants, who will break all the rules. We are both alone in this world, both have a terrible freedom.

They go for a drink afterwards in one of the pubs that looks out over the river. I don't go, I don't like these people. I wander back through the grounds of Winchester Cathedral. I touch the stone. I do this all the time. Every time I walk this way I touch the stone that has been touched by hundreds of millions before me. Sometimes when I'm sure that no one is looking I kiss it. I like to feel it against my lips. I like to feel dead hands against my flesh. Somehow by my contact, by pressing my living body against the stone, I can give eternal life to those who have marked it before me.

'How did your thing go?' Andrea asks when I get in.

'Audition,' I say.

'Yeah, whatever, how did it go?'

'All right,' I say. 'What about you, how did things go in court for you?'

'I ain't been to court yet. I ain't going for ages. They just took me down there and went on at me a bit.

Fucking pigs. Gave me a good breakfast though.' She cheers up at the memory.

'What did you get? You lucky bitch.' Di is almost jealous, almost wishes it was her, not Andrea, who has spent the whole morning being hassled by the pigs.

'Full English, gave me an extra sausage as well. Kim, did you get your giro today?'

'Yeah.'

'Get us all fish and chips, would you?'

'All right,' I say. 'But I ain't going down there. You'll have to go.' Andrea looks as though she might argue, decides not to, gets up and hauls herself out of the door.

'I'm pregnant,' Di says.

'Oh, congratulations.'

'Cheers,' she says.

'What'll you call it?' I ask.

'Dean if it's a boy and Lacey if it's a girl.'

'You'll have to go to Sussex House,' I say.

'I know, it won't be forever though. You'll come and visit, won't you?'

'Course I will.' But I know that I won't. Not for very long anyway.

'Yeah,' she says happily. 'Andrea said she'd visit. She can come and stay up there, if I get a big enough room.'

'What about me? Can't I stay?'

'Come on, Kim, you don't want to stay. It'll be a fucking miracle if I see your face up there at all.'

'Don't be like that, Di, I'll visit you, I promise.'

She looks as though she might cry. I change the subject, tell her about the man in the velvet purple shirt, we both laugh.

Two days later Jeremy, for that is his name, rings and

tells me I've got the part. I feel as though I will burst. Really as though I will burst. I can hardly breathe. I have never felt like this before, didn't know what euphoria was. Di and Andrea take me to the pub for a celebration drink. Whilst we are down there drinking our Malibu and cokes some bird says I'm giving her funny looks. I'm on my own when she says this, Di and Andrea are having a piss. I hope they hurry up. I'm crap at fighting. When they come back I tell Andrea what has happened, the bird is waiting outside for me. Andrea goes out and belts her. Then she comes back in and we have a laugh over how surprised the bird must have been to see Andrea and not me.

'We'll come to every show you do,' says Di.

'Not every one,' I say, although I'm pleased.

'Every single one. You're a mate, ain't you.'

And they do.

For my brother Ben Childs
14.03.1976–26.03.2001
DJ, Free Spirit.
Love always. Until I hold you again.

The Master and the Maid

Jenny Mitchell

This is my day for dying. There's no room in the air, and I'm too weak to laugh any more at the lie that the weak will inherit the earth. I do not want to be touched or saved. But I need someone to listen.

Each night, I am left by the light to dream of Red Tom and my father. I own everything here, but my body is empty; all that can move are the white walls surrounding my bed. They show me a past I would rather not see, that aside from each breath I am dead.

Here, no one is gentle with me. Women charged with my care assault me, lift my head from the pillow too roughly, wash my skin with cold water and leave me to dry in air full of dirt from the fields. I spit out contempt, throat spawn spat at them. They rush away quickly, a hot rage that soothes me. The light is less harsh when they move through the light.

Once, I could force an embrace. Women attended my body with tender attention. I could conjure the feelings and use them obscenely for days.

Now slaves who know nothing, have nothing, come to me here and cry for me dying. The men are the worst. They offer their hats in their hands, lean over my bed and say, Lord save Mas Minton, when I know that wanting me dead has helped them to live.

Men less than me ran to England. I stayed full of rage for Jamaica. England should eat this whole country whole. Sweet-fingered, sweet soil. She would not let me love her. I am not loved. The river outside has a place here, not me.

I remember my wife and her smile that meant nothing. She died in her mouth long before the last breath had finally gone. My son, born too late, sent to England. I was old and impatient and needed a son for this money, no more. He feared me. When strong, I insisted on fear; he rushed to say yes when I spoke.

Red Tom is the man I remember with less than contempt, now that anger and fear are the only extremes of emotion my body has left. He was squat, yellow-skinned, old as me, and red-headed. My father was his. His mother a slave, who died giving birth to our sister, a small, weak-winged creature I am told never cried, too weak for this life.

The day that I want you to listen was young. I was tall for a boy of sixteen. My father, Mas Minton before me, had bearing and I was the same. In rage, he was a man unrestrained.

Only Red Tom attended me after the beatings; I was made to wait days for each one, whilst my father settled accounts, or dealt with recalcitrant slaves.

This day I am dreaming, I was sent to my father by slaves, made to stand in his room. A clock hid in a corner and had the occasional voice of my father. I waited and wanted to ask him to look up and listen but voice would not come. I wanted to say, Father, I am your son, whatsoever sin I've committed only you can forgive.

His voice hit me full voiced. Thief, he said. He knew everything I had stolen – the money I did not need, and a watch I could not sell. I will beat you, he smiled and looked down, his head a low moon. Such delight is not seemly.

My hands held the pain. It was under my skin, itching like insects on fire. Once he whipped me so fiercely, I covered my face with my hands and was handed this pain. It comes every night, all these years later, brought here by such innocent sounds when I sleep, the house as it creaks, a door closing.

My father reached out, placed eight coins in my hand, enough to get drunk with Red Tom. I was told to come back in the dark when he'd beat me; the pain would seem easy, by morning enraged.

Red Tom left his room in my clothes. I said I had stolen the money, and we must get drunk. He laughed his eyes small, chin close to his chest. His laugh always caused me such pain.

We marched into town, drank from one bar to another. Dark came, and singing we walked the road back to the Hall.

Fear made me so small. I cried and begged under my breath, begged into the air.

Tom laughed, then reached out to help me. His kindness, my shoulder, his hand.

I pissed myself crying, a child to a slave who bid me sit down. The whole road was mine. Tom spoke to me, soothing. I lied, insisting his kindness was laughter: how could I go to a beating so soon after feeling such love?

Tom jumped back, showed me the palms of his hands, promised never to mock me. I called him the names I called other slaves, righteous, enraged, a country of piss on my lap. Then I hit him. I knew he must rise or fall down. There was no risk. My defeat would be his; to win did not matter.

Tom fell. I felt the soft sound of resistance, the moan that was breath, and attacked with both feet. I want you to know how it feels: I have walked on the bodies of men; my victory was also defeat.

I know I was beaten that night by my father. He lived to old age, but no image of him survives past that day. Just Red Tom. From then on he obeyed me. Went from Red Tom to Old Tom, then died. I miss him, my brother. Tonight I will see him again. This is my night for dying. I will not be denied.

I say he was no king. I saw him die, I chose the way, and there was little God in him. His body broke, and he was nothing more than crow bait on the bed. That's massa gone. Another one is sure to come.

The whites in Prospect feared his death like pickney 'fraid to lose their father. When he's sick, so many John Crow come to call and bring him pretty favour. When he cannot leave his bed, they stay away.

It's like his weakness makes them vex. They proffer tales instead. At Sunday market, slaves as far as Stony Lea tell stories they have heard about the massa. How he built Jamaica up. With one hand made the land yield forth its wealth. Was worshipped by Maroons but beat them too, until those wildish slaves were scared to burn down Minton land, when they were looting others. They bowed to massa long before the redcoats came, and left that redness on the land.

The stories make me laugh. I know them lies. The only power massa had was wickedness. There was no devil work he would not do and with a smile. They turn him into God by saying he was like the devil. That is how they stay, want-all white people. Massa's dying makes them see, want-all, lose-all, and death will take it slowly.

The day that I was ordered to the Hall, he pulled me close until my shirt in front was open to my throat. His face was covered up in sores. He cried and carried on, and said he did not want a field slave for a maid. I was too old, too rough, too like a man, when that is how I have to stay to cut the cane.

His Doctor Bailey told him he must save his strength, and let me do my best. They know, as all the parish knows, it is my hands that heal the slaves they break up in the crossing and in play. I save as many as I cannot save. They call me Last Stop Queenie.

The doctor told me if I made the massa well, he'd see me free. I promised I would tend the massa like a child, and went to find the herbs my mother knew to make the healing tea.

I held the massa close, until it seems the healing's coming from my breast. He spat and said I smell of dirt, when it is herbs I push inside my hair to stop my fear of him. I want to scream each time I have to touch his skin, and every day my fear turns into rage.

At night the massa sleeps so good. One week with me, his skin is clean, the pain has gone, and house slaves come to wish him well. They anger me, and call me blacky-black, and will not share their food. The men who keep the massa's clothes and tend his stable tell me I must leave the Hall and go to back-a-yard. They wear their owner's broken shoes. It makes them vain.

The house girls sit all day, and follow man. They have such freedom with the massa sick, and let the Hall stay nasty. I would send them to the field. There, overseers carry salt to heal the back-skin they have broken. Cane makes war with hands. The sun beats down to bury we in dirt.

The house slaves have life easy. I let them stay their ways as I'm soon free.

When Doctor Bailey comes again, the massa is so strong he laughs, and says he wants the brown-skin, Twelve, as maid. I must be sent back to the field, as surely I can see I am too precious to be freed.

I cannot speak, but this I know – Twelve is too young for all their nasty ways. I am too old to struggle with the cane.

That night, I let the massa have the healing tea, but I withhold the healing. Morning finds him weak. He calls me, Queenie, please, and turns from everyone but me. The house slaves cannot come to tell their tales. They say I steal the food they grow on good provision land, and take the same to Sunday market. That is so. I eat my share as well, and little girls with pretty hands are made to work as though the massa is not sick. I have his voice, I raise it like a hand.

Soon massa cannot speak. His skin is grey as gully water. Doctor Bailey does not come and stay too long, but tells me I must do my best to ease the massa into death. The house slaves must be free to pay their last respects.

They come at night, when massa cannot move. They cry and bring some light but crowd the room. Their skin is red. They are too proud. The men and women arm in arm the way they see the whites proceed, but dressed in cast-off, hard-washed finery. I watch them from a corner of the room, so sad to see the way they love the massa.

Church Mary bathes him, tender, and says that we

must keep him neat, so God will take him at the gate. When I look close, I see she has the scrubbing brush that she would use on stone. She does not dress him when she's done, but leaves him there to dry in shame.

His man-slave, Devon, tall and meagre, comes to massa with a knife, and cuts his hair so close it raises blood. I know that juju well, and know they mean to do him harm.

Twelve grabs the massa with both hands. Though she is small, she almost pulls him off the bed. Another house slave slaps his face. Each says some word, some curse, their voices deep with pent-in rage.

Then in comes Amine Fall. She is the seamstress here, but given room as though she were a queen. Of all the house slaves, she is dark, and Wolof-tall. She has one baby on her back, another in her arms. The same-day girls are dressed in gold.

She tells us that she stole the cloth the massa meant to line his coat, for Adama and Hawa. Their father, Souba, praised them with the old-time woman names the night that he was sold away, for insurrection in the house.

She turns to massa then, though he is still as death, and says he did not have the right to name the babies here. They had the right to know their father.

I watch her cry. The rage is mine. The room moves closer to the bed. I know they mean to kill him now, and that will see us all in jail, when I have found a safer way.

I push my body forward, make up noise, and raise the juju when I raise my hands. The house slaves pitch me back, and Devon cries that I will save the massa if I have the chance.

I am too strong. I fall on massa's bed, and pinch his

skin. He does not move. I laugh like my old self as when my daughter worked in water, laughing at the way it changed her hands.

I tell them massa's dead. All look afraid, until I say that we must keep it from the fields. The overseers will come hard to put us in our place, and we deserve one day of fête at least. It is allowed that when the massa dies, the house slaves must go wild. Our punishment will come, but not too hard.

They leave the room. I lock the door. We wander first, then sack the Hall, and steal what we can hide in dirt, and drink the massa's rum. The first thing Caesar black-smith does is wear the massa's clothes, and make we call him massa.

Lovers take the time to look each other close and in good light. Young Pan and Giddy go where massa made his books. I watch them at the door. She pulls him close to kiss his cheek, and baby talk. So long, I have not seen so tender.

I go to massa's room, and take more freedom when I sit before his bed. I listen for his breath. He sees me then, and tries to say my name. I will not stand the sound. I raise his head, so he can hear the fête, and die with fear that everything he lived so hard to have belongs to we.

I say my life. My man was Royal. Our daughter Diarra. One sold, one dead in cane. I cry, and then I help the massa to his grave.

Won't leave the body now he's dead, won't leave the room. This is my best. I have helped God, and I will guide the devil.

Fur Coats

Kate Pullinger

'What are we doing tomorrow?'

'Going to Emma's in the morning, school in the afternoon, then Sian is picking you up so you can play with Marcus after school.'

'What are we doing the next day?'

'Going to Emma's in the morning, school in the afternoon, then Marcus is coming over here to play.'

'What are we doing the next day after that?'

'Going to Emma's in the morning, school in the afternoon, then tea and cakes after school, most likely.'

'What are we doing the next day after that?'

Will she kill him? Of course not. But she contemplates it.

In spare moments, Clara thinks about the past, about the time when she was free, before she bowed down to domestic servitude. Is that what it is? She isn't at all sure how to describe her present state. There is one thing that Clara is sure about, though (whisper this, she thinks): *parenthood can be boring*.

Back then, in the old days, Before Baby, Clara lived in a big dingy house with a bunch of artists; she wasn't an artist, but they didn't seem to mind. The big dingy house was one of a collection of big dingy houses around a long-neglected South London square. No one knew who owned the buildings, but they moved in anyway, jimmying the locks, climbing in through the windows, and set about renovating. Clara's house was actually two houses; once they got themselves established in the first house – electricity, gas, plumbing – they knocked through the walls at strategic places, mostly stair landings, and annexed next door. House number two was exactly like house number one, except in reverse, a mirror-image. It made for a pleasing symmetry. One of the blokes expanded his room at the top of the house to include the room next door. His space was enormous and, consequently, perfect for parties. They had lots of parties.

Her own room was small and cosy, with a tiny fireplace and enough space for a table and chair and her single bed. Clara liked the narrow bed, with its worn black and pink blanket; it gave the room a spartan appearance. She'd stripped the floral wallpaper off the walls when they moved in, and had left the old plaster bare; she liked the look of it as well, the meandering cracks, rough and smooth, glazed and dull like an old leather coat you might find on a skip. The artists would have made the bare walls an aesthetic choice, but Clara left them untouched out of uncertainty – what were you supposed to do next? She stuck postcards of her favourite paintings low on the wall, where she could gaze at them as she lay in bed, but these fell off within a few days, wedging themselves down between the skirting board and the wall, leaving tags of bluetack in their place.

She kept the room warm – warmish – with a paraffin heater. It sat in the corner like a pale green metal chimney pot; it was fumey and unreliable and if she had it on for long she worried it might explode. But it was better than nothing, better than the unrelenting cold.

And so Clara and the artists concerned themselves with the business of living – crappy, low-paid jobs in retail and catering, signing on, eating cheese on toast late at night after the pub, endless talking. The artists were concerned with Capitalism and its Onward March through time and space; they were concerned about the World and Politics. Margaret Thatcher was in Downing Street and they felt a profound unease, casting around for a foothold against Nicaragua, apartheid, Israel. This was what occupied the artists at the kitchen table, this was what they discussed at the pub, this was what they argued about while falling in and out of each other's beds. Clara listened in; she was like a highly-tuned listening device – like a spy, in fact. Except she wasn't a spy, she was just Clara. She was waiting for it all to make sense.

He is four years old. Tall, and getting taller. Very independent, and yet dependent too, traces of babyhood lingering. Sitting on his mother's lap is still a priority at times. And his mother's opinion looms large. 'You've hurt my feelings,' is his favourite complaint, along with 'I'm very cross with you,' and 'I'm very upset.'

'What are we doing tomorrow, Mummy?'

'Sweetie, we've been through this. You know what we're doing. You do the same things every week.'

He looks a little crestfallen.

'What are we doing the next day?'

'I don't know, sweetie. Where's your bag of dinosaurs? Have they all escaped?' At four, he remains divertable.

*

One of the big dingy houses on the square had its ground floor converted into a café. They took it in turns to produce big, healthy vegetarian meals – large trays of vegetable crumble, lasagne, apple bake. Any money raised went toward a cause; there were many causes, and the causes needed money. Everyone came along, to sit at the stubby old tables on the wonky chairs in the candlelight, bringing their own beer and wine, and the conversation wove itself in the air, like a rich and delicate textile one of the artists had designed.

Clara didn't know anything about the Iran/Iraq war; she didn't know anything about El Salvador, she'd barely heard of these places. They were very far away. None of her housemates ate meat and some of them took this particular tenet as far as not wearing leather. Clara had a couple of pairs of strappy leather slingbacks stuffed under her bed; sometimes when she was in town she would buy and eat a Big Mac. One of the artists had been to Nicaragua and was raising money to go back; another was dodging the South African Army draft; another had gone to prison for the ALF, the anti-fur, anti-vivisection brigade. Clara had had a teddy bear childhood in Teddington, south-west London; the house she grew up in backed onto the Thames. In summer, Clara and her brothers used to swing out over the water on a rope, letting go to crash into the silky warm river, carefree dive-bombers with no known enemy. Church of England, a girl's school, a Mummy who stayed home and baked cakes for tea: this childhood was like a basket she carried around at all times, full of good things. Because of it she would never go hungry. But it weighed her down as well, with its narrowness, its politeness, its concern with courtesy. No matter what she wore, no matter what colour she dyed her hair, it shone through:

her parents' affluence, her way of speaking. She felt a barrier between her self and the rest of the world, not only far-flung places but the artists, her friends.

This is what he likes to eat: pasta, sauce free, garnished only with a dab of pesto from a jar and a sprinkle of cheese. Sausages. Cheese sandwiches. Little baby tomatoes, cucumber. Mango. Bananas. Broccoli on occasion – unpredictable. Same for fish fingers. Nothing resembling grown-up food, nothing where the flavours are mixed or complicated. He eats well, providing she does not attempt to spring anything new on him. And of course he loves sweet things. Every little sweet thing.

Sometimes he can be exceptionally graceful and charming. One evening as she is getting dressed to go out he points to an item of her clothing. 'What's that?'

Clara looks. 'A skirt.' She doesn't get out much these days.

And later as she is putting him to bed: 'Mummy, you do look lovely.'

She almost cries. 'Thank you, sweetheart. Thank you.'

Their relationship has an intensity that is heartbreaking. It marginalises everything else. There he is, so little and sturdy, with his hopes, his dreams. How could he be anything other than demanding?

Clara didn't have a cause of her own. She wasn't that way inclined. There was too much choice: what was it to be the homeless in London or the disappeared in Chile? It all felt too pressing, too urgent, too desperate; and besides, she thought, perhaps the world would be destroyed in a nuclear holocaust anyway. She contemplated joining CND; she contemplated joining many things.

And sleeping around. Clara didn't do that either. No particular reason, it just wasn't what she did. The artists didn't expect it of her. 'You're too earnest,' they would say to her, as if that alone ruled out sex. 'Isn't it important to be earnest?' she'd reply. And she'd laugh and the artists would look at her as though she came from another planet.

And then the miners' strike started. Up north somewhere. Up there.

As the strike took hold, the Left mobilised ('The left what?' Clara wanted to ask but did not), and with it, the artists. In the square, activity coalesced around the café; they held a meeting to discuss how to fundraise. The miners were asking for food and money. The artists decided they needed someone to lobby the manager of the local supermarket. Heads turned. Clara swivelled in her chair to see who was sitting behind her. But there was no one. They were looking at her.

'But,' she said.

'Clara,' they replied.

And so she applied herself. She wrote a letter to the manager first, and then made an appointment by telephone. She wore a suit that one of the artists had helped her find at Brick Lane market; it was older than she was and cost fifty pence. She put on lipstick and when she looked in the mirror she thought her mother had suddenly appeared. She put on her strappy leather slingbacks and told herself it was in aid of a good cause. Then she trudged up the broad gusty road, rubbing grit out of her eyes, batting away flying crisp packets. Under the rail bridge, to the right and into the supermarket. She was so nervous she had to remind herself of her own name.

'We would like to hand out leaflets at the front entrance to the store,' she said.

The manager nodded and smiled.

'The leaflet will have a list of products that your customers can buy for the miners and their families. Food, toiletries, household items.'

He smiled again, encouragingly.

'We will be at the exit to collect the products as your customers leave.'

The manager remained pleasingly silent.

'We will be polite and discreet. Cash donations may also be given.'

At last the manager spoke: 'Sounds fine to me.' He smiled again, his benevolent, managerial smile.

When Clara got outside the supermarket, she screamed.

He can make her angrier than she'd thought possible. How was she to know that motherhood would make her so angry?

'I won't!'

'You will.'

'I won't!'

'You will.'

They are discussing the picking up and tidying of toys.

'I won't!'

'You will.'

He throws himself on the floor and wails. She struggles to suppress her own rage, like forcing a vengeful genie back into a tiny bottle. He is four, after all, he no longer bites, kicks, or pinches, so why should she?

'I'll help you.'

He stops sobbing as abruptly as he began. 'All right then,' he sighs wearily. 'Come on, Mummy.'

When he's asleep it is easy to love him. He sleeps with his arms flung out, blameless, abandoned to it, so far gone sometimes he rolls right out of bed. She lies awake in the next room and listens to him when, at two a.m., sometimes three, he gets up and, standing, drinks from the glass of milk she has left him, puts it down, goes to the loo, gets back in bed. At these moments she doubts her own perceptions – is she no longer the person she used to be? Has motherhood, with all its responsibilities, with its abrupt shifts in way of life – one minute she's party girl, all sheeny and bright, the next she's in on her own every single night – changed her as much as she thinks?

The supermarket collection went well; the supermarket's customers responded with thoughtful generosity, supplying much more than endless tins of baked beans. And they were well organised in the square, ferrying the goods to the central collection point on time, constantly amending and updating the list of requested goods according to instructions from the NUM strike committee. Clara listened to the radio news reports with interest, wishing they had a telly. The strike had many factors against it: the power utilities had enormous reserves of coal, the Nottinghamshire union did not go out on strike, there was no secondary action. Arthur Scargill had not balloted the NUM, and the artists debated the wisdom of that night after night around the kitchen table. And there was Thatcher herself, astride the country with her pearls and her hairdo and her voice.

Delegations of miners began to arrive in London. They came down to attend rallies, to help mobilise and fundraise. There was plenty of room to put up people in the big dingy houses around the square and so they notified the strike committee. The artists began to organise a special benefit night in the café, a welcoming party for their guests. As the day approached, the square was buoyant with anticipation; it was not every day that the Cause came to stay. The delegation was from a small mining town outside Manchester; none of the artists had ever been anywhere near the place. As far as Clara was concerned, they could have been coming from Namibia. She had never met a miner. She had never seen a miner, nor a mine, nor even a pit village. In fact, the closest she had come was reading Zola's *Germinal*, a novel set in France during the nineteenth century.

Finally, the evening was upon them. Everyone gathered in the café.

At 8.30 they put the food on the back burners. At 9.00 they started to open bottles of wine. By 10.00 dancing had broken out in the middle of the café. By 10.30 some people could wait no longer, and the kitchen was raided. By 11.00 they had forgotten why they were having a party. No one noticed the minibus arrive.

The door of the café opened. Someone shouted 'shut up' and the music was switched off and everyone stopped dancing, eating, drinking. Clara stood on a chair to get a better view of the door, and she gasped in spite of herself.

She had never seen so much fur.

They had been expecting a dozen miners. What they got was a dozen miners' wives.

They trooped into the café one by one, taking up an enormous amount of space. No one had anticipated how much space they would require; every single woman, every single wife, was wearing fur. Fur coats, brown-red and silky, silver and glossy, black and shimmering; fur hats, bulky and soviet; one woman was wearing fur gloves. The café's inhabitants took a collective gulp. And then someone shouted 'Welcome!' The miners' wives smiled. 'Come in,' someone else shouted and, with a laugh, 'can we take your coats?'

The thing about having a small child, Clara finds, is that it forces you back into your own past, into your own childhood. It makes your parents into people – people like you, in fact. It is that negative bind that characterises so much of parenting – at Clara's worst moments, when she is too tired, too harassed, too not-herself, she thinks: I'm turning into my mother. And then she thinks: Is that such a bad thing?

'Mummy?'

'Yes, sweetie.'

'What are we doing on Wednesday?'

'Wednesday?' Today is Thursday.

He nods.

'Emma's in the morning, school in the afternoon.'

'What are we doing on Friday?'

Ah, she thinks, he has moved on a stage. Is he trying to impress me with his grasp of the days of the week?

'Friday is your swimming lesson.'

'Oh,' he says, 'that's right. I'm very good at swimming.'

She doesn't reply, she is attempting to tune the radio.

'I'm very good at swimming, Mummy.'

The damn thing has a terrible hiss.

'Mummy, I'm very good at swimming.'

She can't get it to work. It's been like this all week.

'Mummy—' he is getting louder. 'Mummy—'

She succeeds in her fiddling. At last she hears what

he is saying. 'Yes, sweetheart, you are very good at swimming. You should put your face in the water next time, shouldn't you.'

He nods, pushing his train across the carpet. Now he isn't listening to her.

Clara couldn't understand a thing that the miners' wives said. Their accents – specific to the village in which they had lived and worked all their lives – were unintelligible to her. The woman they had staying in their house was called Barbara; whenever Clara encountered her on the stairs or in the doorway she smiled broadly, said 'Hello Barbara,' and then scuttled away. She got on with her supermarket collecting.

In the evenings Barbara wore her fur coat and held court in the kitchen. The kitchen had no heating, but Clara and the artists had grown accustomed to it. When it got too cold to bear, they turned on the cooker and left the oven door open. While Barbara was staying, the household undertook to cook a good meal every night. The artist who grew up in Leeds, Mark, served as unofficial interpreter.

Barbara said something.

'Do we always eat together?' Mark translated. He also supplied the reply. 'Well, pretty often, I guess, maybe even most nights. We take it in turns to cook.'

Clara was sitting in the corner, hoping she wouldn't be called upon to speak.

Barbara said something.

'No, we don't have a cleaning rota as such.' Mark looked a little shamefaced.

Clara looked around the kitchen. She realised, with surprise, that it was filthy. On the floor the lino was cracked, missing in patches. The walls were festooned with ad hoc wiring and the wires were coated with oily black dust. There was no splashback behind the cooker and the area was dark with grease; the wall behind the rubbish bin was caked and streaky.

Barbara said something and then laughed warmly.

Mark smiled. 'Yes, we do have big hearts.' Everyone in the kitchen either guffawed or giggled and Clara smiled in spite of herself.

Another two days and Barbara and the artists were beginning to comprehend each other more fully. One morning, on her way to a rally at Westminster, Barbara came into the kitchen while Clara was making toast.

'Would you like a piece?' Clara offered.

'No thank you.'

Clara spread vegemite on the bread, despite not liking the taste. She thought it might be good for her.

'It is very kind of you to put us up here in the square,' Barbara said.

Clara shrugged, she didn't know how to reply.

'Things are tough in the villages now. We are running out of money.' Barbara put her handbag down and began to button her fur coat. 'No more overtime bonuses. I might even have to sell this!' She spread her arms wide and laughed, then was abruptly serious once more. 'I worry that we are running out of time. Our whole way of life – it's not nice down the pit, but—' she stopped herself. 'You know all of this already.' She smiled again. 'You people obviously have nothing.'

Clara put down her toast and looked around. And then she realised that Barbara thought they lived this way because they were poor. Nothing to do with choice.

'And yet you have been so generous. We appreciate it so much. All over England, people have been—fantastic.'

'It shouldn't be happening like this,' Clara said. She

meant the strike, she meant the pit closures, she meant
the violent battles on the coalfields between the miners
and the police. The plexiglass-clad police.

'Ah,' said Barbara, 'but it is. It's not the young men
that I worry about; they'll be all right. It's the older ones
that'll end up on the slagheap—like my Robbie.'

Clara couldn't reply.

'Okay,' said Barbara, breezy once more, 'I'm off.' And
with a soft and furry flourish, she departed.

It has been an awful morning and it looks set to get
worse. It has been raining since they got up – hard, silent
rain. He has a temperature and a runny nose and she's
worried he's got conjunctivitis from rubbing snot into
his eyes. He won't lie down and he won't play with his
toys. Instead he follows her around the flat and whines.
She has a cold too, and a hangover from the three bottles
of beer she drank last night, in front of the telly. All she
wants to do is lie down and be very, very quiet.

He whines.

Now she is brittle with tension, close to cracking. On
days like this he's not a little boy but a huge force, a
tremendous non-stop barrage of need.

The phone rings. She leaps up and answers it.

'Hello love,' Barbara says. 'Are you up for a visit this
weekend?'

It is fifteen years since the strike – fifteen years, Clara
reflects, as she listens to Barbara speak. After the
strike Barbara's husband Robbie took redundancy and
promptly died. Their kids were grown, so Barbara went
to college on the redundancy money. Now she manages
an enormous supermarket in Manchester.

'I'm thinking of taking the fur coat out of storage.'

Clara laughs.

'No, listen—they're back in fashion—they're all the rage.'

'They are not.'

'They are! It says so in my magazine.'

'Oh well then.'

'You're young, you look great whatever you wear.'

'I'm not young anymore.'

'No?' says Barbara. 'I suppose not. How's the lad?'

He is sitting next to Clara on the settee, his head in her lap. He takes her hand and places it on his temple, so that she'll stroke his hair. 'He's all right,' Clara says, 'he's okay.'

The Night Shift

❧

Georgia Moseley

As soon as I walked out of the airport I was mugged by the fleshy heat of a Californian summer evening. I took off my pack and leant against the entrance in the warm blue dusk, speckled with neon. I could just make out the skyline in the distance. Adverts surrounded me, offering glimpses of what lay before me. Across one billboard a fifteen-foot-tall tanned torso curled across a bottle of Chanel No. 5, wearing nothing but a bikini made of her own strategically placed arms, and a plump pout; next to her a young couple with white teeth tipped their heads back in gleeful unison with two small Kools cigarettes jutting out bonily from their hands. Even the dusk light was hyper-real; the sky glowed and the air throbbed with the gentle hum of machinery as it was conditioned, cooled, and slipped back amongst us. I felt as though all of America must somehow be plugged into a power outlet. It leant towards me, like the proverbial strange man offering you sweets, and I took them.

A month after I arrived in Oakland the nation settled into its collective armchair for the long Labor Day weekend. I still knew few people there and so, armed with a pitcher of whiskey sours, I planned to spend most of it slumped in my rented apartment, watching the Sergeant Bilko TV marathon, and avoiding the heat.

I had been lying on my couch for some time when across the flat roof outside my window I heard the hurried clip-clops of pointy heels heading my way. I heard a scuffling and then a tiny brown hand reached through the open window and hauled a body onto the sill. ''Ello, my friend! Its me, Dolores!' I got up and pulled aside the curtain. Crouched on the sill was a small woman in a tiny, shiny dress and sparkly heels. She had a fedora on her head and winked at me.

I had met her briefly in a history class a few weeks ago; she lived a few blocks away and occasionally dropped round on her way to the city. It was appropriate that I should meet Dolores in a class called 'The History of American Consumption'; she devoured life, eyes blinking in bright lights, swallowing up tales, shaking out dances, and always getting invited to the lavish and mysterious events of people she barely knew. 'Darleng,' she addressed me and extended a just baked leg into my room, then another and she stood there on my desk and rolled a cigarette before walking to the edge and jumping onto the floor, leaving dusty footprints on my work and letters home. I took a couple of steps backwards and sat in a chair.

'I'm going to the city – I know this great little bar that makes fabulous margaritas! Come with! Come with!' and she stamped her pointy foot and lit her ciga-rette. Her foot stamp turned into a repetitive slap-slap-slap and then dragged its pair into a wild tap dance. I watched her from my slouch on the chair. She danced in and out of the curtains waggling her hat at me.

'Okay,' I said, one eye still on Bilko, and I pulled a shoe towards me with my toes. She was already in the closet and throwing clothes at me. Dolores favoured fancy pieces, slices really, of silky stuff, in deep colours and fur-rimmed. I struggled into the bits and pieces and she bound the concoction together with a trickle of a belt that clung to my comfy hips for a second before it shimmied to my feet in a noose. I started again.

'This!' she exclaimed, holding up a furry-collared leather jacket by the scruff of its neck, 'is inexplicable!' She slipped it on over the sequinned dress that she was wearing and pulled her fedora over her eyes and climbed back out of the window. I watched her totter across the flat roof beneath my window and leap from the edge of it with a squawk. I waited for a bit, hunched on the sill then I too jumped off; ran stumbling across the flat roof, and followed her uphill towards her badly parked car that had been left with its engine running.

Evenings in San Francisco darkened slowly in late September. It was after ten and the last of the sun was diluting into smudgy orange and then deep blue above us. I stared through the car window as white wooden buildings, tangled trees and cream dogs blurred past. The details of American life are perfectly edited together through the half-open frame of a slow-moving car window. The moment when a wide-sided woman bends down in her stretched pink skirt to finger a fat foot in a too small shoe, and looks up at you, her glasses glinting in the dusk light, for a second we register each other, and then both glide by. At the lights, as the sun went down, a skinny man wrestled, sweating, with a toilet bowl on the sidewalk in front of a neat house. Standing on the lawn, hands on hips, a middle-aged man watched him, while his wife stood on the porch, hand up, hiding from the last of the sun.

'It's gonna have to come out,' said the wrestler.

'What?' asked the lawnman, 'the whole john?'

There was a warm pause, and as the lights changed

his wife said, 'Are you sure?' She stepped off the porch, and raised her voice in panic, 'Are you sure?' And we disappeared round the corner.

We were in Dolores's grandfather's old Buick. It had one long blue plastic front seat that we slipped about on as we surged along, the fraying seatbelts flapping next to us. The seat was cracked beneath my legs and I picked at the foam that was exposed. Her grandfather had died a few months earlier, leaving lots of dust, lots of shoes, an unexpected cache of old love letters, and the car. I had never met him and she didn't tell me much, but I was building up a picture of him.

Dolores had kept the car exactly as it was when he had it, except the back seat was piled with her laundry; she was always on her way to or from the launderette. I never asked but it seemed that the pile never actually left the car now; it was impractical, I suppose, since everything ended up back there anyway. The front and rear windows were trimmed with a string of tiny black pom-poms, a rosary hung from the mirror, an inch of Romeo y Julieta cigar sat squatly in the ashtray, and a creased picture of two laughing kids was tucked into the sun-shade along with a peacock feather. They were dressed up as fast food, the older one was wearing a milkshake suit, the younger one strapped into a foot-wide box of fries. Dolores glanced over at me.

'I'm the fries,' she said, and returned her glance to the road as she pushed her foot down on the accelerator. I slipped my arm into the slack loop of the seatbelt, and tried to get it to lock into the holster without appearing too nervous. Nothing happened; no reassuring click. I hung on to it for a while then tied it to my belt. I rolled my window down as far as it would go, and the warm evening air rushed in. I rested my head on the door and looked out; the sky was so high, with American stars glinting far above me. Dolores flicked on the radio, lit a cigarette, and we were sucked onto the freeway.

We sped along the 80, Dolores slapping her hands on the steering wheel in time to the music that drifted in and out of reception, occasionally jumping into snippets of Glen Miller's 'Chatinooga Choo Choo'. We glided left, took the exit for the Bay Bridge and ran parallel to the water for a while where we merged into streams of traffic from the left and right that once on the bridge kept their distance from each other. We took the first exit. Dolores grabbed the cigar and held it between her molars and squinted up at the road signs.

'We're looking for the Hotsy-Totsy Club, so eyes wide, darleng.' We drove up and down a street lined with old shops that alternately housed ancient barbers, fried chicken cafés, and new-looking coffee bars.

'We're not exactly where I thought we were,' she shouted at me over the radio. I reached across and twisted the volume, suddenly Benny Goodman shrieked into the car from a cloud of static. We both jumped, and I turned the knob the other way. 'Ah!' she shouted, 'there it is.' She made a U-turn and pulled up next to a small building with a neon sign above it that said *Hots* in red and beneath it *otsy* in green with *cl b* added much smaller along the bottom as a smooth pink afterthought. It was next to an old warehouse, which had *www.suck-myassyouyuppiescum.com* sprayed along the top of it. 'This is what City Hall calls a *transitional* neighbour-hood.' She opened a black handbag revealing a scarlet lining, and pulled a lipstick from its guts, applying it perfectly with her eyes closed. 'The old community is being squeezed out by the new businesses – dot-commers mainly. In five years this whole place will be different,' she said matter-of-factly. She adjusted her fedora. 'Okay, darleng?' I nodded and we slammed the car doors behind us.

Inside it was dark; the bar was made from a large wooden boat that had been cut away at the back to allow room for the bar staff. Above it hung three lamps made out of the crispy ballooned shells of different dried fishes, each with a light bulb suspended inside. They glowed gold through their spindly skins, occasionally turning slowly when caught in the slipstream of a passing drinker. The walls were coated with hundreds and hundreds of business cards that had been stapled to them, most now yellowing and curved. To the left of the bar was a giant grand piano, on which rested the few drinks and many chubby arms of the patrons that were seated round it on stools. They were singing 'Edelweiss', led by a well-stuffed-looking man in his late fifties who wore a dark blue shirt trimmed with ruffles, tucked deep into his trousers. He sat playing the piano and singing into a mike that had been attached to a pillar next to his head using lashings of brown parcel tape.

Dolores and I sat in a booth opposite the singers and a large blond barmaid in her fifties came up to us; her thick ponytail swung left to right like a metronome. 'What can a getcha?' She had a little mustard on her blouse, which strained to keep up with her body's shifts and rolls.

'What kinds of margaritas do you have?' I asked. She hid a yawn behind her notebook.

'Lime, fancy lemon, regular lemon, cherry, strawberry, and house.' She rolled her gum to the other side of her mouth. 'Pitcher or glass?'

'A pitcher of the house, thanks,' replied Dolores, and stretched out on the seat. The waitress wrote something in her notebook and then stuffed it in her waistband and left.

I examined the business cards that created a browning fringe to our booth. An ancient add for a mechanics had a hand-written addition in capitals: 'TAXI SERVICE'.

Dolores lit a cigarette and tossed the match into the ashtray on our table. 'This place has been here years. My grandfather told me he used to come here in the forties. Back then it was really *the* place – well that's what he told me. But he prefixed most things with *the* when he talked about the old days.' As she spoke her hand wagged wildly; I watched the glowing tip of her cigarette dart about from the corner of my eye. It was sweeping ember arcs back and forth near the wall. I looked around; tiny pieces of crispy paper were flaking off the walls and chafing with sixty years of powdery dust, and hundreds of bottles of methylated-looking spirits gleamed at me from behind the boat-bar. I looked about for the fire-exit.

Suddenly the singing collective broke out in a vigorous song, which involved one person singing the main part, only to be interrupted by the rest of the group singing 'Mother, may I?' in unison every two lines. This chorus was accompanied by a finger-wagging gesture, which they all did to each other with gleeful enthusiasm. An old man in the booth next to us looked over at them, shook his head and said to us, 'I'm about ready to take a little vacation.'

'Where are you going?' I asked politely.

'Sleep,' he replied and leant back into his booth.

A few drinks later and Dolores and I had been squeezed in around the piano, and while Dolores joined in with the show tunes, I was clamped under the arm of a generous-fleshed woman in a blue muu-muu who proceeded to probe me about why I'd come to the States. When I told her I was studying she nodded.

'Yes, well, though I do hair by day, I have been at art school for eight months. My teacher could immediately tell that I was talented: that I was an artist.' She drained her Snowball and crunched on an ice-cube. 'After four months he said to me, "Melly you are ready for a show. London, Paris, New York, you name it." ' She leaned in to me, conspiratorially, 'At first he thought I was a French expressionist, but then he realised he was wrong. Turns out I'm a German expressionist. Who knew! Oops, here's my line,' and she turned back to the group and spilled her falsetto across the piano.

We left as the first bars of 'Guys and Dolls' were breaking out. The old man next to us had woken up and was dancing the waitress slowly round the room; when he dipped her his wide lips pressed into a smile. 'Hey Ray, my hair is touching the floor!' she exclaimed and pulled her back up as they laughed. The air was still warm outside and we walked towards where we had left Dolores's car. 'God dammit,' Dolores stood exactly where the driving seat would have been and folded her arms. I looked up and down the street, maybe it had just crept a few metres up the road while we'd been inside, trying to sneak home without us.

'Should we call the police?' I asked, sitting down on the curb.

'It's the police who have it. It's been towed. It's probably at the Hall of Justice over on Southside.' She turned and walked back into the bar, and returned with the Jim Costello mechanics card and went to the pay phone across the street, jangling some coins in her palm.

She is pretty persuasive, and though Jim Costello had

passed on seventeen years ago, apparently there was still some kind of a taxi service, and they sent someone out.

Our taxi driver smelt warm. He was a young man with a nervous hairdo – each piece was standing up and out as far apart from the rest as possible – like it was trying to flee his head.

'Hall of Justice hey? Not a problem.' He held the steering wheel in one hand, and a portable TV in the other, which he kept moving to try and get a reception. 'Oh yeah man, they tried to tow my tail once. I was lying in bed in nothing at all. Some dude pounds on my door, he's all, "Hey, dude it's street cleaning – they towing your car." ' The picture sharpened and the show *Who Wants to be a Millionaire?* fizzed into view. It had no sound but he kept one eye on it anyway. 'I got up and just ran down there, like I said, I was buck naked. Hey, I know this one!' he shouted to the TV, '1492, right? Or 1692? Err, anyway, and these dudes, they were hitching my car up to a tow-truck and I just climbed in the driving seat and started her up.' He glanced in the rear-view mirror, changed lanes and then stepped on the accelerator. 'She didn't go anywhere of course – the front wheels were in the air spinning round. But I just kinda drove it there on that spot until they put it back down. Fuckin' bullshit that was, but it taught me a lesson – if you naked enough you can get away with most anything.' He swerved to avoid a car. 'Hey, asshole! Do you see me? Do you goddamn see me?'

We drove up and down steep hills lined with huge wooden houses, each painted different colours, violet, pale blue, yellow, and a bistro on every corner. At the traffic lights we waited as a group of men and women in evening wear crossed, gaffawing to each other. 'God this neighbourhood is just slathered in opulent butter,'

Dolores sighed. Running alongside us was a purple Chevy that had two bumper stickers, HOW'S MY DRIVING? 1–800–EAT-SHIT and, above that, YIELD TO THE PRINCESS. By now I had folded myself into a comfortable half-piece on the seat. I turned my head to the side and smeared my cheek against the cool glass.

'We're drunk,' Dolores announced for no reason, her head bobbing next to mine. Our driver looked round grinning. 'Hey, so am I!' he replied proudly and punched the air with both hands, for emphasis. We all laughed. After a while I rolled upright; I had no way of knowing if he was taking us the right way or not. I looked around aimlessly for landmarks, my eyes swinging from building to building in the half-light; I couldn't read the landscape in this town the way I could at home, and eventually I gave up, and my eyes slid disorientated down the side of a flat-fronted office building and returned to the road just in time to see a tunnel mouth stretch wide in front of us. As we sped into it the taxi driver leant forward a little, his stomach pressing against the steering wheel, I leant back, and then the tunnel swallowed us all.

Our car exploded into noise as the engine joined others echoing round and round the walls of the tunnel. It was lit with ill, pale orange lights that striped through the car every other second as we passed under them. I watched him out of the corner of my eye as we rattled through. He was staring ahead, his profile alternating between a one-dimensional silhouette, and being lit up, his features soaked in neon. In the rearview mirror he caught me staring, and smiled. We burst out of the tunnel and the cab was flooded with cream streetlight again

He was offering us a drink from a brown-papered bottle when we pulled up outside the Hall of Justice. We stood on the steps and watched him leave, shaking a wave to us out of the window. Inside it was like every government building in every city across the world – beige and brown gloss paint with worn burgundy lino. We walked through the corridors until we found the towed cars office at the end of the *Lost and Found* hallway.

It was lined with benches that were holding an exhausted mess that had been spat out from various bars in the city. On the wall were posters recruiting for the police force, and a large notice listed the charges and the acceptable forms of payment – Visa, Master-Card, check, or cash. Beneath it someone had written 'or donuts' in black pen. Dolores queued while I sat on a bench sobering up. I read yesterday's *Chronicle* and watched the careless car-less drift in and out.

By the time the sky was beginning to lighten around the edges we were back in the car and joining the Bay Bridge. To our left the whole city lined up to watch us leave; thousands of tiny yellow windows faced us, every one a square millimetre of condensed life – layers and layers pressed behind each one, and the whole lot gone in a blink. Dolores had tied her hair up in a turban and was driving tired, with one leg up resting on the dashboard, pink painted toes pressed against the glass like cherries preserved in a jar, sipping from a 99 cent SuperBigGulp. Ahead of us a line of red tail lights sloped slowly out into the night, leaving behind a lazy purr.

That was the last trip we took in that car; by the end of the month it had broken down irreparably. For the rest of that year Dolores kept it on her front lawn, and when I came over she'd often be in it, listening to the radio, or sorting through her laundry. I explored the rest of the city on my own; walking for miles through different neighbourhoods, down the length of Market Street, across the wrong side of town, the right side of town, watched the leaves turn brown, fall, and mix to a mulch, held under glass by the first frost. I was always moving through the city, and it seeped into my shoes. Of all the things I keep with me that moment comes back the most – when I looked down over everything from the car that night on the bridge; the pom-poms mid-swing, a jar of cherry toes on the dash, and a thousand lives lit up around me.

Killing Guinevere

Fiona Curnow

The allotments were next to the graveyard. Allotments usually are, Ray thought. Cosmic recycling – growing and death? Nah. Probably more to do with where the council can get cheap land.

He swung his good leg over the low slate wall, dragged the other one and started down the path. Old men with hoes made a big deal of not looking at him. On one of their ex-front-door sheds he could just make out the ghost of where he'd felt-tipped, *The tygers of wrath are wiser than the horses of instruction*, one pissed-up night two years before. There had been a letter to the local rag about it – how young hooligans these days couldn't even spell.

Sion was working his plot at the far end. He was unsnagging brittle pea stalks from green netting and throwing them on the barrow.

Pea stalks, Ray thought. When I first came here I wouldn't have known that's what they were. It would have just been 'green stuff'. Now I know he's going to compost them and fold the netting up for next spring and make sure he doesn't plant peas or beans on that bed for a couple of years. Funny life.

'Si!' Ray called. 'Need a hand, mate?'

The older man straightened up. Slowly. He looked at Ray for a moment.

'Wondered if we'd see you again, boy. Where you been?'

'Walkabout. Hopabout. Not far, like. Just over the border – Shroppy, mainly. Weather's turning a bit iffy for living in the bender now. Thought I'd come back and crash at Jonno's for the winter. We go way back. He owes me.'

'That blow in. He brings you down, boy. You could do better.'

'He's a mate with a roof. I need one right now.'

'No flesh to keep the chill out, that's your problem. Been living on cold baked beans and black coffee all summer if I know you. Here, get something decent in you tonight.'

Sion bent over and twisted up some leeks from the next bed along. Then some carrots. A little earth clung to them – crumbly, dark, hard won from the grey mid-Welsh clay by ten years' persistence. He pulled a Kwik Save bag from the pockets of the tweed trousers he always wore. They might once have fitted him. He bagged the vegetables and handed them to Ray.

'Thanks, Mum. Where's Gwen?'

Sion's eyes narrowed. Ray wasn't sure if he'd gone too far with the 'Mum' quip. Sion knew full well he hadn't seen his folks in Brum for years. Not since the motorbike accident. And things hadn't been brilliant even before then. He'd told Sion about that too – one day last January when they'd sorted through brown envelopes of seed and passed a hip flask back and forth to keep their fingers from freezing up. Or maybe the old fella was still particular about people using his bitch's full name.

'She's . . .Come see for yourself. She's in the shed.'

Sion left the barrow where it was. Ray followed him to one of the typical allotment sheds that bloomed, fungus-fashion, one from each patch. Green, paint peeling and built of whatever had come to hand. They looked like children's play pretend houses.

A shopping trolley took up most of the free space inside. In it was a blanket. The blanket gave the impression of being alive. Not so much the movement. There was hardly any. After a while Ray realised there was a very slight breathing that didn't even disturb the rank, grey wool. Sometimes the breathing would pause for a few seconds as if it had run out of impetus.

Ray turned back a corner of the blanket. The wolf-hound's head shifted. At the other end of the trolley the blanket twitched. The tail thumped. Just once.

'She knows it's me,' Ray said. 'Guinevere. Jesus, Si, what happened? She's only a young dog.'

'She's been going downhill for a while now. Few months ago, I was petting her one evening and I felt a lump on her belly. Thought nothing of it. She was still herself. You know how full of life she can be. Could be.'

'Tell me about it. If she hadn't floored me, spring before last . . .'

No, Ray thought, if that great pup hadn't bounded up and knocked me over when I was taking a short cut through the allotments. If you hadn't apologised and come over and offered your hand to help me up. If I hadn't said, 'It's okay' and started explaining about my dodgy leg. If it weren't for that great raggy wolfhound you'd never have spoken to me. You'd look at me – or not – the same way all the other old men around here do with my Saesneg accent, my dreads, the rings in my face.

'I kept an eye on it,' Sion went on. 'It got bigger. I began thinking I should take her to the vet. But she still had that spark in her eye. I thought, there can't be too much wrong with you, girl. Kept putting it off. Kept thinking, next week. When my pension's through. When the leccy's paid. I let too many "next weeks" through. Last Saturday morning I came down and found her like this.'

'Man, you got to take her to the vet. I'll help.'

'No! It's too late. If I take her in this state they'll say I should have brought her months ago. That I've been cruel. Neglected her. Take me to court, they would. Happened last year – fella over Rhayader way. Banned him from keeping another dog for life. Not that I'd want another. Not after Guinevere. But the shame, see, Ray? All them people in suits standing up and saying I'd been cruel to her. I love her. You know that. She's all I've got. I wanted to keep her by me – long as I could. What do I do, Ray?'

Sion looked up. His eyeballs fitted into his face like his body fitted into its tired old clothes. At the corners of the baggy sockets was a moistening. Sion had never asked Ray for anything like advice before. Come to that, he'd never used his name. It was always 'boy'.

Ray patted the long wiry head. Guinevere's eyes stayed closed though her tail beneath the blanket twitched again.

'She's beyond knowing where she is, Si. We've got to do it for her. Do what the vet would do.'

'How? I've thought about it. But I can't. Not when it comes to it. I couldn't have done it for my Alice at the end. Wanted to hold on to her too, see? I can't do it for Guinevere.'

'I'm back now. I'll help. What about your nephew?

You said he got the family farm. Farmers always have shotguns.'

True, he added to himself. I've been poked awake by the barrel of one in the small of my back more times than I'd like.

'You taking the piss, boy? I can't.' Sion touched the dog's domed skull. 'Beautiful, she is. Even when she's ill. I won't have a mark on her.'

'Plastic bag over the head? You've always got dozens. She's in no state to put up a fight.'

'I thought of that. Night before last. Went through 'em all – found a Marks and Sparks one. Thought, there's classy. Sat by her for an hour with the bloody thing in my hands, just stroking her head and telling her it was for the best. Couldn't do it. No dignity.'

He laid a hand over the dog's unresponsive ears. One tear trickled from the crepey outer corner of his eye.

'We shouldn't be talking like this in front of you, girl. Listening you are. It doesn't seem right.'

'Sion, if you took her to the vet he'd give her an injection, right? Be like going to sleep. Is that what you want?'

'Yes, but—'

'Leave it to me. No – don't ask. We won't do it here.'

'You're right. It should be special.'

'Meet me back at your house in fifteen.'

Sion turned the corner of the blanket back down to cover Guinevere's head.

'Didn't want anyone to see her like this. And the trolley was the only way to get her about. Expect folks think old Sion's finally lost it.'

Ray opened the shed door. Then he realised something. He turned back.

'Sion, where do you live?'

*

It was a quiet street. Middle of the day – no children playing, no cars going past. Just a couple of old men walking their Jack Russells or some other small, appropriate breed. One man was leaning on a front gate. He was speaking to his pal. They stopped as Ray went by. They might have known one another fifty years, Ray thought. But they still leaned on front gates to talk. He'd bet they'd never been inside each other's homes.

Fifteen minutes, he'd told Sion. By now it was more like forty-five. He'd decided to pack. Didn't take long – he'd only just got here. Jonno had been well out of it when Ray had slipped his hand, tooth fairy-like, under his mattress to get at his works. Then he'd taken Nev's – from the hollowed-out space under the resin Buddha. Jeez, so obvious. It was best to be sure. Guinevere was a big dog. But ripping off both guys? Better pack.

Sion was watching for him through the obscured glass front door.

'Thought you'd changed your mind, boy.'

'Sorry. Needed to get some stuff together.'

'You need a ghetto blaster for this?'

'No one's called them ghetto blasters since about 1988. Where is she?'

'Back room. Always liked to lie in that patch of sun by the door, she did.'

Ray followed Sion through, put down his stereo and shrugged off his rucksack. Guinevere was lying on a rug. Not the stinking grey travel blanket that had covered her in the supermarket trolley. This was a bright rag rug like the barge folk made. Her fur was damp. The room smelled of baby shampoo. Sion must have given her a bath.

'Good, man. You've done good. Let's get some candles lit. And fetch us a clean teaspoon.'

Sion had some candles on the shelf above the gas fire. How long since they'd been lit? Ray wiped the dust off and arranged them either side of Guinevere. He found some more in a cupboard. Plain white power-cut ones. He made an arc of them behind her. Her breathing was slow and moaning. He knelt in the space he'd left in front of her and took Jonno's tin from his rucksack. It was the type a child's geometry set had come in. You could still see the picture – set square, protractor, compasses. At thirteen Ray had tried to pierce his ear with a compass. The green stuff had kept coming out for weeks.

'Here's your spoon. Anything else?'

'No, man. Just say goodbye while I'm sorting the stuff. She's hurting, Si. Not fair to make her wait.'

He shuffled back to give Sion some space. He would have plugged in the stereo to give them some music but the wall plugs were the round pin type. The wiring in this place was that old? Must be a death trap.

To hell with it – let's do this properly, Ray thought. It's only batteries. Guinevere deserves some music to go out.

Afro Celt Sound System was in the tape deck. He turned the volume low.

'All said I was mad, they did, when I got you,' Sion murmured in his dog's ear. 'Getting a pup like you at my time of life. And a big breed too. The way you ate! Selfish of me, I suppose. Always wanted something different, I had. Something outrageous. Alice would never let me, see? The children were all hers. Sensible names. Anne, Robert, William. I wasn't trusted. So when she'd gone and I blew the last of what we had on you, I called you what I damn well wanted. The kids called me a daft old sod. And not teasing like the boy here would say it. Guinevere, you were the only thing that was ever all mine.'

He kissed the wiry cheek and sat back.

'You ready, Ray? You can do it now.'

It took three goes to raise a vein on the bony foreleg. Then Ray eased in the hypo. It took a few moments. He wondered if he was going to have to use a second shot. But the breathing was becoming shallower. It was difficult to pinpoint the moment it stopped. Sion stroked the dog's head. He was smiling.

'There's dignity. Thanks, boy.'

'Let me fix you a cup of tea, man. Or – no. I've got a better idea.'

Ray undid the breast pocket of his denim jacket. There was a spliff ready rolled in there. He'd meant to smoke it down by the river on his way back from the allotments. He lit it from a candle and took a few puffs to get it going, then he handed it to Sion.

'Take it in deep. Hold it there a moment. That's it.'

The old boy was getting the hang of it. For a few moments all he did was smoke. Dead dog. Candles. One old man. One young. The dim back room had a strange feeling to it. Ray realised what it was. This was the first time in five years he'd sat down in someone's home and felt wanted.

But his fingers began to twitch. Doesn't he know he's supposed to hand it back? he thought. Hey, give the guy a break. He's just lost his dog. About to lose the other stray he likes to take care of. This is no time to get heavy about spliff etiquette.

'There's none of my kids I could have asked to do this,' Sion said after a while through smoky outbreaths. 'All live in London anyways. Good jobs. You understand, Ray. You thought a bit about Guinevere, I know you did. Glad it was you. Glad we're friends.'

Friends. In the year and a half he'd known Sion they'd never used that word. It meant something.

'What are you going to do with her now, Si?'

'Don't know. Hadn't thought that far.'

'When I was staying in the woods this summer I got talking to this guy. He told me about sky burials. It was a Native American thing. You expose the body on some high platform and the birds come down and pick it clean. Take everything back to the Great Spirit. Very natural.'

'I don't know. Round here you'd have the council on you for that. I don't know about burying her in the garden neither. The house isn't mine. Probably something in the lease against it.'

'Cremation?'

'Last time I lit a bonfire folks next door had environmental health round. I'm on my last warning. No – I'll take her back to the allotments when it gets dark. Tuck her in under the compost heap. Damn thing needs turning anyway.'

'She'd like that. She was always sniffing in it.'

'Recycling, innit? That's what we're all supposed to be doing these days. When I reckon my time's up I'll crawl in the heap myself. It's warm. It's dark. There's worse places to go. You see them brassicas haven't been weeded for a while, boy, and you'll know where to find me.'

'Don't think it'll be me comes looking for you, Si. Need to make myself scarce again.'

'You just got back. Somewhere warm for the winter you said. We were just getting . . . comfy.'

'You didn't think that gear we used was mine?'

'Didn't like to ask.'

'I nicked it. Only do a bit of blow myself. And that started mainly for the pain.' He patted his thigh.

'They bad?'

'It's the cold. There's that much metal holding things together. The doc said, "Ray, you ever go through one of those metal detection archways at the airport you'd better warn them first. The alarm'll go crazy." Me. In an airport. As if.'

'You could try my nephew. The one with the farm. If you need somewhere to stay for a bit. Not far out of town but I'm sure no one would come looking for you. I'd ring and tell him you were coming but they cut me off week before last. I could write you a letter to give him.'

'You're all right. This has got me thinking. Might hitch back to Brum – look up my folks. It's been years. Maybe even sit those "A" levels I never got round to – what with the crash.'

Sion leaned forwards and clasped his hands.

'You're a good boy, Ray. You deserve to do something with yourself. Guinevere would be glad.' He took back one hand and stroked the dog's still head. 'It's getting dark. I'll take her back down the allotments. Give me a hand getting her back in the trolley?'

Outside the front door Sion said, 'You get them leeks to your Mam while they're fresh. She'll do a better job cooking them than you could.'

He turned and trundled off towards the far side of the church.

He didn't say goodbye, Ray realised. Perhaps he doesn't like saying it. Perhaps he thinks if he doesn't say it it'll work like a charm to bring me back.

It had been a sweet lie to tell. It had made Sion happy.

Even now, pushing his dog towards her resting place, maybe he was imagining Ray in a centrally heated flat being hugged and back-slapped with Brummie warmth. The Prodigal returns. Yeah.

He picked up his stereo and hefted his rucksack onto his shoulders. His leg didn't like the extra weight. He could have done with those crutches. Why had he been so fucking proud about them?

Something was dripping down his upper arm. He'd shoved Sion's vegetables, in their Kwik Save bag, on the top of his rucksack. There had been rainwater in the leeks. It was seeping, muddily, down his arm.

The house at the very corner of the road had battered ride-on toys in the paved front garden. Ray hung the bag of vegetables on the gate latch. They could be seen from the front window. Someone would spot them when they came to draw the curtains. Might as well go where they'd do some good. No way to cook them where he was headed.

It was dark on the way to the plantation above the town. Ray's torch batteries were low. He hadn't thought he'd need them again so soon.

The plantation was warmer than the bare hills. Mindful of the dangers of resin Ray cleared a space in the fallen pine needles to build a fire. His stereo batteries weren't too healthy either. But he turned *Afro Celts* up as high as it would go. No one to complain out here.

He wanted to dance. It had been so long. He remembered the summers he'd sat round camp fires, watched others reeling to bodhran and tin whistle. He'd stayed on the ground, kept time with his hand against his good thigh, sucked like an angry baby on the bottle going round and asked himself again why the hell he'd gone pillion with Jonno that night when he'd known the state his mate was in.

'I'll do it for you, Guinevere,' he said. 'I'll dance for you. That's how I'll see you out.'

All crazy limbs and crazy shadows round the fire. He wasn't used to this. His left leg stabbed each time he stamped it on the needled earth. But the pain was something. Fierce. Pure. It kept him in the here and now. If it got too much there was always Nev's gear in the side pocket of his rucksack. He'd only needed Jonno's to send Guinevere on her way. Pain wasn't the only option.

A Wrong Thing

A.L. Kennedy

I would prefer not to open my eyes, not this morning. In the end, I know I'll have to, but I'll do it against my will. I would much rather not co-operate.

And the insects, they don't help. They're outside, I've no clue how many, but apparently a lot, and all of them are making these hot, unpredictable scuttles of noise, like chafed tin, loosed wires, there beyond the walls and windows, thousands of tiny instincts signalling they want to kill each other and have sex.

That's fine, though; they're not in here with me, at least I don't think so. I have no desire to check.

But I would like to know why my mouth tastes of rust, which means iron, which means blood. I hope I've just eaten rust and forgotten about it; hardly likely, but I'll try to believe it, anyway. Last night, I must have swallowed something rusty, or licked it, and now I don't recall, can't yet recall. And I think I had a dream with metal in it: perhaps it's possible to save a flavour you've known in your sleep.

I have definitely saved a bad feeling of some kind, another aftertaste, and both of my eyes are still shut, because I am nervous about them being any other way. Even so, it will be okay, not unpleasant, completely familiar, when I break out into my first look at the day.

I can do that: it isn't a threat, shouldn't be a threat, there shouldn't be anything untoward about it.

Shuttered windows, slicing jabs of light, the bed beneath me bobbing briefly like a dinghy on a lazy sea. That isn't right.

There you are, though, seeing – no problem, nothing to worry about.

Except for the bed and the light, which is far-advanced, the kind that you only get when you've missed the morning and I didn't think I had. It also hurts, which it really shouldn't. Deep in the meat of my brain, something I can't identify has become extremely sensitive and, tucked away beneath all this, my teeth feel unfamiliar and my tongue is, somehow, in the way.

My bed bobs again. I wish it wouldn't.

But this is not a problem: it is a solution, in fact, because now I understand the bobbing, the bad feeling, the trouble with my eyes, the rust: I am not well.

I am not well and in a foreign country.

So I should think about insurance and if I took any out and what class I might come under – negligence, poisoning, infection, act of God – I'm not exactly sure how I will qualify.

I don't want to see a doctor.

I'm almost certain that I dreamed about a doctor, one I didn't like. Sleeping or waking, there's no way to tell here if someone really *is* a doctor, if their needles are clean, or necessary, if what they say they'll do to you is safe. So I'll go without.

I am in a foreign country and sick.

My legs are sticking to the sheets, I notice, everything about me showing obvious signs of being over-heated, feverish.

Nice word, feverish. You couldn't guess its meaning.

I did think I was cold, but apparently I'm not. Skin under sweat, it's meant to look attractive. It doesn't – it blotches and drags, seems furtive, unclean.

This will be the photograph they use, post-mortem – distasteful areas boxed out under black – and then there'll be the holiday snap – here she is, when still living – the unwittingly poignant smile. The papers will show them both for comparison. Or maybe I'll only make it to the internet, uncensored.

Anyway, I don't have a holiday snap. I don't take them. I don't want to see and no one else does, either.

A pressure fingers underneath my heart and my mouth fills with saliva. Swallowing is difficult and doesn't help, I have to wipe my lips which I find are now oily, unfamiliar, vaguely obscene. I reach behind my head, unsteadying the edges, the corners, the meeting places of the ceiling, walls, floor. I catch at the air conditioner's control and turn it. The mechanism jolts and then begins to grind out a minor disturbance in the padded warmth above my face. Without intending, I picture vast wheels milling, hidden by the plasterboard, crushing the limbs of something, wet tufts of hair, lodged and oozing in the cogs.

No, imagine nice things, kind things, happy things, cool water, cut grass.

Frost. Frost on a field: a meadow, better word, meadow: and a little, frozen river under trees, well-intentioned trees.

The pace of my saliva relents and the weight in my stomach shifts, sly, but then settles, not unbearable.

I could lie on the river, roll out flat, naked, cheek to cheek.

I have a clear, soothing sense of frozen water, the slowly melting nubs and flats of it, moulding to me, and my panic is resting back, dwindling, until the idea of ice reopens last night's dream.

I was ill there, too: in a hotel room, a bathroom, the bathroom I have now: grubby white tiling walls, truncated tub, everything the same. Trying to sit up in the bath and the ice chips sinking underneath me, creaking when they shift, lifting my hands which are thick with cold crystals, brownish pink.

The mirror opposite me seems to fluctuate and pitch. I may have brain damage. I may be hallucinating. I may be unable to tell that I am not.

Then I hold still and everything else does, too.

Somebody told me this, or I read it: the story where you wake up in an ice bath and, taped where you can see, there's a note which says you shouldn't stand, shouldn't even try to, that everything is over and done with, no point in being alarmed.

'Good evening, Service.'

Out in the corridor, a pass key fidgets at the lock.

Good evening, what?

Louder, 'Good evening, Service,' the door sweeping open and, almost immediately, jolting to a stop. I've left on the security chain – being a nervous traveller comes in handy at last.

What time is it, actually? The staff here say the same thing to anyone English-speaking, night or day. Here it's both good and an evening perpetually.

'Service.'

I'm going to start bleeding somewhere, if he keeps up that noise.

'Come back.' I have to swallow again, 'later.' My voice sounding masculine and strangled. 'Please.'

'Service, good evening.' The door nudges in again experimentally, but gets no further.

What the hell is 'Service', anyway?

'I am not well. Come back. Tomorrow.' My stomach cramps slightly, teasing.

He'll understand, 'tomorrow', surely to God.

'I clean room now, please.' The voice doesn't sound insistent, only certain of how things are done.

'No. You clean tomorrow. To-mor-row.'

God, I sound like a racist. Bellowing things, demanding. I mean, I respect other cultures, I try, but I do only have this one language, which is a failing, but what can I do. I want to sound agreeable, I truly intend to.

'Service. I clean today.'

'Oh, will you just *fuck off!*'

Jesus, I'm sorry, I'm absolutely sorry, I completely am.

There is a wounded silence in which I do not audibly apologise. *Well, I didn't ask for 'Service'.* Then the door flinches shut, the lock clacks, and I don't feel remotely relieved because of this kicking which blossoms through my torso, and raises a fresh, throbbing sweat. If I don't reach the bathroom before I exhale, I will vomit in my bed.

Funny how you always want your mother when you're throwing up. No matter what.

Funny.

And let's do this properly, first time – clear and finished, please.

So think of the note, the dream of the note – you're shivering and reading that surgeons have taken out both of your kidneys, they've drugged you and stolen the pair, and then sewn you up, empty and dying and packed round with bloodstained ice. You haven't been murdered, your body will kill you: slowly, because you've been chilled.

And this works like a nasty charm, clears more than everything. While I shake through the last, hard coughs I move my hands to check my unaltered back. I'm still complete.

Tim was there in my sleep, too. I remember now, seeing him turn his head, as if I'd called. He was sheepish and excited, at the edge of smiling: the way he'd always be while he waited to see if I knew that he'd done a wrong thing: when he wanted to check we were both going to like it, make it allowed.

My throat feels ragged. But the spasms have flattened and subsided: I do seem better.

I finish the last of the bottled water, rinsing my mouth and then sipping. *Avoid dehydration – it creeps up.* Beyond the windows, I hear thin, repeated screams from what I guess must be a bird, something anxious and predatory, ascending to my left. Walking evenly, as if I might spill, I go back to the wreck of my bed and then lie down gently.

Tim would have enjoyed this.

Not that Tim welcomed illness for itself, he just wanted to take care. It's what pleased him: padding about with aspirin, hot water bottles, snacks.

He would take off his glasses and we would understand that I was just better enough. He would take off his glasses and put them beside the lamp, pull the covers back. He would take off his glasses and blink, be free then to lower his head, his clever mouth.

I am breathing through my teeth, trying to keep the memory angled away and to have no feeling. This isn't a time when I can afford to be disturbed.

Sometimes I would just pretend, go upstairs and draw the curtains, fighting fit and waiting for his mouth.

This is unwise.

When Tim was ill himself, though, he preferred to be left alone – like a cat, he said. Then I found him on a Sunday morning, early, in the kitchen, and I told him he didn't have flu, that it was serious, and then the first doctor finally arrived and talked to me as if I was a child, said house calls were reserved for emergencies, but after that, Tim was trying to walk and falling and talking to nobody, until I made a second doctor come, with an ambulance on its way, because I'd described Tim's rash again and made them understand that he had meningitis and might die.

Might die.

But I knew he wouldn't.

They shaved his head and trepanned him to let the pressure out. In three places, they drilled through his skull and he was alone with them when they did it. But, when it was finished, I sat by his bed, stayed there talking, saying his name for days while he was still. I kept calling him in. I was sure he wouldn't go, that he couldn't leave me.

He came home two stone lighter and with a soft stubble on his scalp, a dressing. And he had a new skin: fierce and pale and naked, completely naked. I couldn't see him without touching him. At first, only with my mouth, because that was gentle. He needed gentleness.

I move my head to study the telephone; like the rest of the room, it is behaving normally. I could use it to call Tim. The time difference, though, the other differences – it would all end up being difficult.

While he lay on the hospital bed, I made him promises, more than I can remember, I put all that we might *be into his silence, his sleep. Sometimes I think it's made me a disappointment for him since, made him regret what he found when he came back alive.*

I roll on my side and set the walls and carpet swinging, my head is muzzled suddenly, held in something wet. I retch, stumble up for the bathroom and retch again.

When I kneel, I don't touch the toilet – *no need to volunteer for other illnesses* – I breathe between the rising cramps – *Oh Jesus, oh Jesus Christ* – and I want my mother. *Fuck*. Another series of jolts. *Oh, fuck it.*

And nothing happens, not a thing. In what must be half an hour, I bring up a single, scouring mouthful of bile. Whatever this is, I can't be rid of it.

Back on the bed, I crouch, defensive, enormously hot, and reach for the phone. In a quite unlikely but persuasive way, it seems both more beautiful and more solid than it did before: a worryingly lovely, heavy telephone with a button to press for messages – *I either haven't got one, or it doesn't work* – and one for reception and one with a symbol I don't recognise – *God knows* – and one with a tiny waiter and tiny tray – *which means Room Service. Not 'Service'* – **Room Service** – *that's what I want.*

'Yes, Room Service? I need water. Please.' *I have no water left,* 'Large-sized bottle; bottles. I want two large-sized bottles of water.' *Without it, a person can die.*

The line out to wherever Room Service is prickles and whines.

'The biggest size.'

I have no idea if I am audible, or understood, 'I have not been well.' *As if they care.* 'Sorry . . . Can you? – Sorry. Water . . . Water?'

There must be guests who can do this, who find it easy, who can just order things. 'Sorry. Two bottles.

Please.' *Without making a single apology. Or saying please,* 'Two bottles . . . Hello? Good evening?'

The connection oozes away, to finish in a tiny click.

If Room Service never arrives, there will be no water. I need water. If Room Service does arrive, there will be water. Which I need. But then I will have to get dressed and stand up and unlock the door and reach out and get the water, carry it. I don't know if I can.

Now, even when I close my eyes, something undulates – the blood light at the back of my eyelids, it's treacherous. If Tim was here I would tell him that, or would have told him, before the meningitis and the disappointment.

It was that time, that evening, weekday evening, when I walked in on him and watched his face close, everything blurring to neutral, to a chill, just because I was there. I had surprised him being the way that he used to be, but it wasn't for me anymore, so he shut it away.

We spend more time working, he takes evenings out, it surprises me now when we meet in the house; going into a quiet room and there he'll be. I try to look irritated and leave before he does. We go on holiday without each other.

I flatten myself to the sheet, press and press my forehead against the small creak of the mattress as if this will alter a single mistake I've made. Because I didn't shout, didn't grab him by the arm and shout in his face, didn't throw a clock I was fond of and hurt to see it smashed and to see him keep on going, leave the room without a sound – I didn't do any of that until it was only stupid and too late. An infection in the brain, the doctors told me, might make him different and so I went against myself and drifted for months, let him be, let what I knew of him go.

Except when that light comes back to his skin, that nakedness. Not to talk, not to see each other – it's only to meet his mouth, lace my hands behind his new, cropped hair, know we can taste what hasn't changed.

'Room Service, good evening.'

The door stammers with a series of knocks and I am caught in the cold recollection of lying beneath a husband I can't speak to, both of us dead weights, breathing, recovering ourselves, our sadness, our embarrassment.

'Room Service, good evening.'

'Yes.' I am still naked. 'Yes. Good evening.' And I don't want to move. 'Leave it outside the door.' I don't want anyone near me.

'You want—?' It isn't the would-be room cleaner, I think I would recognise that voice.

'I said, leave it outside the door.' *And if I sound like a colonial oppressor, I don't care.* 'I can't get up now. Leave it.'

'Good evening. Thank you.' This sounds slightly put out, but a muffled clunking gives me cause for hope.

I will stand, I will wrap myself up in the sheet and do what I must to get my water.

When my hand finds the child-skin at the small of his back, I always wait for that.

My scalp tingles, as if there were someone behind me, or above, and the insects worry on and I lever up to sit, then stand. My balance swims, but lands again and I drag the sheet round to cover me, shuffle for the door.

The lock foxes me for a moment, no more than that. I open it, lean out into the hot, empty passageway, swipe down for the two bottles, retrieve them and half stagger back. The effort of this bangs in my head. Still, I have my water – that's fine.

*

'Good evening. Good evening? Room Service?'

The line is a little worse than before, as if it anticipated my call and is already disapproving.

'Yes. I ordered water. Two bottles of water and you left them.' If anyone is listening, they make no sound. 'Someone left them . . .' *This is too complicated.* 'Someone left them and I have them, but the seals on the bottles are broken . . .' I wait for an intervention of some kind, but none is forthcoming: I will have to say this all on my own. 'If the seals are broken . . . by mistake.' *There's no reason to accuse anybody – obviously that's what I'm doing, but I don't really mean it that way.* 'I can't drink. I have been ill. All day ill. I need clean water.'

'Our water is clean.'

'I'll . . .' *Shit.* 'Look, I'll pay for new bottles, but if the seals—'

'I will send him again.' The distant receiver clanks down.

So I'll have to be ready when he arrives.

Shit.

I move to look at my jeans where they're crumpled on the chair, moderately baffling, and then lift them, scattering meaningless, small coins out of the pockets. Methodically, I balance, step, waver, then work my way in. The T-shirt is easier. After that, I stay on the chair, waiting, smoothing my breath, ducking every thought of Tim's hands, the way they can be, confident and familiar with fastenings, the parting slip of cloth.

More quickly than I expected, the knock comes.

'You have a problem.' He is perhaps seventeen, lost in somebody's oversized guess at an impressive uniform: cuffed black trousers, a purple jacket with gold piping, creased patent leather shoes. 'There is something wrong.'

He makes each statement critical and precise, a slight edge there to emphasise that he can understand my language while I would be lost in his.

Well, I'll apologise for being British later.

'I, ah, yes. The seals . . .' *This sounds so petty.* 'I'm sure this has nothing to do with you, maybe your supplier . . .' *His sleeves are turned under to fit – and he sees that I've noticed.*

He sets down two new bottles of water on the table and lifts up the old, unwilling to admit defeat. 'The seals . . .?' He delicately twists both caps, then waits until I meet his eye, so that he can break off and make it plain he is examining me, the tangled bed, the slovenly room, the indications of deeper disorder.

I try to sound brisk, 'The seals are broken, as you can see.' *I should have put on underwear – then I might have a sense of authority.* 'That will be all.'

'Our supplier is at fault. I am so sorry.' *His insincerity is entirely calculated.*

I will have to sit down soon, 'That's fine then.' The young man shows no sign of moving.

Well, I'm not giving him a tip – not unless it makes him go away.

His hands are shaking visibly. I suppose that he might be afraid, either furious or afraid, perhaps both.

'Thank you. I'll tell your manager you've helped me. Good evening.' I attempt a smile, but he ignores it and leaves with a pointed, 'Good afternoon.'

Maybe I've lost him his job.

Or maybe everybody down in Room Service spends their days filling water bottles from the tap, from stagnant pools, from beggars' wounds, how should I know. We've made them suffer, why not? I probably earn his year's salary in a week.

I don't care, though. Not one of them is my responsibility.

The new seals are okay, the first one giving with a reassuring snap and letting me, finally, drink. It tastes faintly chalky and lukewarm. I run a few drops into the hollow of my palm and wipe my face.

Next year I'm taking my break in Europe, in Britain, at least, then I'll be poisoned close to home. Tim never goes far: a long weekend in Antrim, the Lake District, a few days in Argyll, the Orkney Isles. He always comes back happy. Because he's been away from me.

But if he's happy, that's when he'll do a wrong thing.

I keep drinking, probably too much.

Lips against lips while I stroke his hair, feel when he breathes, swallow when he swallows. Clever mouth, it always deepens the parting, opens it, smoothes the smooth. And then he looks up, lifts his head: Tim, sheepish and excited, at the edge of smiling. It used to be the little glance that made sure I was happy and he was allowed. Now it lets me know that this is wicked and nice because we are two strangers.

When the telephone rings, I rush a mouthful, cough.

No one but Tim knows I'm here.

'Hello?'

'Good evening. This is a single occupancy room?' It is a hotel voice, a stranger. 'It is single occupancy?'

'It's *what*?' I am conscious of the liquid weight I've loaded in.

'It is a single occupancy, what you have paid for.'

'Yes. Single. Yes.'

I don't want to deal with this now – whatever this is.

'You don't let our personnel clean your room. You have been there for the complete day, not leaving. Now you have two bottles of water. But this is a single occupancy room.'

'Look, what are you . . .? I've been ill. Ill.'

Room Service – they're paying me back.

'I need a lot of water.' There is a sceptical pause. 'You can come and search if you like.' And another. 'Two bottles doesn't mean two people. I mean, if I was in the same bed with someone, we could surely share the same bloody bottle.'

This is obviously a deeply improper suggestion, 'I have to ask if you are alone, this is all. This is my job.'

'Great, you've done your job. *Good evening.*'

I hang up, before they can say anything else.

And fuck you. Single occupancy. What else.

Then a twist of nausea shakes me, doubles me forward. Arms, legs, everything is slippy, jerking with each lunge, and I don't think I can walk and I am right, but I tumble and crawl into the bathroom, the cooler floor, the business of being freed from this.

It takes a while.

And then something has altered. The stillness is more definitive. My lips seem tender, I am lightheaded, but I know I won't have to be sick again.

Found the trigger, didn't I.

Some thoughts are best left quiet and I shut myself against them every day. It isn't often that they have a use.

But today they were what I needed.

So I unlocked the morning when I smelled it on his hands and chose to ignore it, believed I was wrong, until it was there again one night, there on his face, his mouth, his lips: the scent of a stranger, of some other woman, some cunt. Tim, he noticed when I flinched, and took

care to kiss me again, as if he wanted me to be quite
sure that he'd done a wrong thing.

And I was sure enough to picture it, the way he would
look up, happily caught in the act, before he tongued
back in. And I knew that he wouldn't leave me and that
I couldn't leave him.

I still know it now, the way that I know my name:
Christian, Middle, Married. It won't change. And, more
than any infidelity, it sickens me. It sickens me.

I wash my face with bottled water and I stand. The
room is itself and I am me. Nothing has changed.

Yanks

Jo Campbell

Unity lay flat on her back on the pavement by the postbox, with Bonzo on her chest. Her underneath was cold, but the April sun was shining on the top part of her and Bonzo had lost so much stuffing he was more like a furry blanket than a dog. If she squeezed her eyes tight and then opened them a crack, she could make tiny rainbows shimmer and dazzle through her eyelashes. To one side, at eye-level, were two pairs of feet: Mrs West's sturdy brown boots planted solidly apart, her mother's high heels making little fidgety movements as she talked.

Their voices were different too: Mrs West's slow and sticky, like condensed milk pouring, Mummy's lighter and quicker, a tap splashing; together they made a tune that Unity listened to with pleasure. What they were talking about was not interesting: that was why she had lain down.

There was a lull in the voice-music.

'Your Americans are still with you, I see,' said Mrs West.

'Yes. There's still no news.'

'It must be nice for you to have the company. Two jeeps outside till quite late the other night; quite a little party.'

'I try to make their friends welcome. They're a long way from home.'

Mummy's voice had gone funny, flat and stiff.

'So many are, my dear, these days. Have you heard from your hubby lately?'

'I had a letter last week. He was all right when he wrote. Couldn't say much, of course.'

'Well, I'm sure he'd be glad to think that you're having some fun while he's away.'

'Good heavens,' said Mummy, 'look at the time, I must be getting home. Where's Unity? Get up, you silly girl, you'll get filthy. So nice to talk to you, Mrs West.'

Mummy walked fast, her high heels clicking on the pavement. She was cross, Unity could tell from the way she held her hand, tight and hot. Was it because of her lying on the pavement? She lagged and pulled against the grip.

'What's the matter now?'

'You're going too fast – your nails are digging in.'

'Don't whine,' but Mummy slowed down and relaxed her hold.

For as long as Unity could remember there had been just her mummy and her. In other houses there were brothers and sisters, like Mrs West's May and Arnold next door, and daddies who came home at teatime. There was a picture of Unity's Daddy, in uniform, on the mantlepiece in the lounge, but Unity didn't think he was quite real. Nana and Grandad, who lived far away in London, were more real; Mummy wrote to them nearly every day. Most real of all were the American nurses, Pat and Beth, who had been living with them for ages now, and the friends they brought to the house.

Indoors, Unity watched as her mother took off her

little flat hat and changed her street skirt for a pair of green slacks.

'Your clothes are nicer than Mrs West's,' she said.

'Well, I should hope so,' said Mummy, laughing a bit. 'They were London things, in their time. Come on, let's go and get the tea.'

On the landing they met Pat, coming out of the double front bedroom that the two women shared.

'May I have a bath, Mrs Sherborne? Chuck's picking me up later.'

She called it a ba'th.

'It isn't a ba'th, it's a baarth,' said Unity, but Pat took no notice.

Mummy looked at her watch. 'Half an hour,' she said. 'I'll stoke up the boiler. And if Beth's in she'd better use the water after you.'

'That's fine, Mrs Sherborne, thank you.'

Of all the Americans who came to the house, Colonel Robertson – Chuck, but Mummy said it was rude to call him that – was Unity's favourite. Although he belonged with Pat in some way, Unity knew he really came to see her. He would call out to her as soon as he got in the house and then they would play wonderful giggly games together, or he would ask her to teach him how to talk English, or sometimes he would read her a story while Pat stood waiting to go out. Colonel Robertson had strong arms that could whirl her round and round, and a hard chest: his eyes wrinkled up when he smiled, and he smelled of ironing. Pat had dark hair and eyes, and a little line of dark whiskers on her top lip. She smiled a lot, but her eyes weren't kind. Unity didn't think she'd want Pat for a nurse, if she was a poor wounded soldier, and she couldn't see why Colonel Robertson had chosen her.

'Don't know what he sees in her,' muttered Mummy in the kitchen. She put on her rubber gloves and hefted some coke into the Beeston: she opened the flap at the bottom and worked the poker to and fro with a scrunching noise. A few cinders fell on the kitchen floor and a small cloud of fine dust drifted up. Mummy swept up and smacked her hands together.

The Americans came after tea: Colonel Robertson, Lieutenant Hancock, who was big and noisy and belonged with Beth, and Major Kerr who didn't belong with anybody but came anyway. They brought Unity sweets, which they called candy, and chewing-gum that Mummy didn't like her to have. They said they were going to drive to a pub outside town, and they invited Mummy, but she said no, she had to put Unity to bed. So Unity played in the garden with Colonel Robertson while the girls got ready and the others talked to Mummy. Behind the racket she and Colonel Robertson were making Unity could hear their voices drawling and twanging, her mother's voice replying, bright and rapid. Once she saw the three of them standing with their heads together, and guessed they were looking at photographs again: mothers or brothers or sisters in America. Mummy always asked questions and said how pretty the girls were, even if they weren't.

The lawn where she played with Colonel Robertson was the top bit of the garden where the flowers were and the two horrible chickens, with raw necks and untidy feathers, in their wire enclosure. Two big apple trees screened off the bottom end where her mother had planted rows of peas and beans, seedling lettuces and radishes, tomatoes and potatoes, digging and raking vigorously in her green slacks and a pair of Wellingtons, and swearing beneath her breath at slugs and birds and weeds. Unity loved the garden, and was not a bit surprised when Colonel Robertson asked politely if the Americans could hold their picnic in it 'because we don't know any place better'.

They had been planning the picnic for some time, just waiting for the weather to be good enough. Unity thought eating out of doors was a lovely idea, and had been very disappointed when at first Mummy had turned down an invitation to go: she said it wouldn't do. Then she bit her lip and said she was caught, but she said yes all the same.

The day of the picnic was a beautiful fine Sunday, the hottest day of the year so far. Mummy hunted in the airing-cupboard for a clean tablecloth, and put out rugs and cushions. The men arrived about twelve o'clock, their Jeeps laden with cans and packages. Unity had never seen so much to eat: chicken legs and tinned meat, sweets and biscuits, cheese, jam, peanut butter and a big glass bowl from the kitchen filled to the brim with different kinds of tinned fruit. Mummy made tea, and orange squash. May and Arnold next door watched jealously through the fence. 'Go tell those kids to come in,' Colonel Robertson had said, and she had, but their mummy wouldn't let them.

Unused to choice, Unity didn't know how to choose, and ate too much. She felt full, and fruit syrup had spilled down the front of her best dress; it was wet and sticky on her skin. Although having dinner in the garden had been fun, there seemed to be something wrong: everyone was a bit quiet and dull. She had done her best to liven things up; she had recited all the nursery rhymes she knew and sung her songs and asked riddles, until Mummy hurt her feelings by saying, 'That's enough, now, Unity; don't show off.' Now Colonel Robertson and Pat were sitting on the grass at opposite sides of the white cloth. They hadn't eaten much, and they both looked sad. Lieutenant Hancock and Beth were under the big apple-tree, their backs to the trunk; he had one arm round her and was drinking beer out of a can.

'Play with me?' said Unity.

'Later, maybe,' said Colonel Robertson. 'Right now I have to talk to Patricia.'

He stood up and held his hand out to Pat. She looked scared, but in the end she took his hand, and they went indoors together.

Unity was bored. 'Where's Mummy?' she asked.

Lieutenant Hancock had slid down on the grass. His eyes were shut. He had put down his beer and his arm now lay across Beth's lap. Beth still sat upright, her legs in their sheer stockings stretched out in front of her. She had kicked off her shoes.

'I guess she took Dan to see the runner beans,' said Beth lazily.

Lieutenant Hancock chuckled.

'Stay here, honey, give your mom a break,' said Beth. 'Come over here, I'll read you a story.'

Lieutenant Hancock made a funny moaning noise, and Beth slapped his hand and giggled. Unity knew they didn't really want a story, and she felt offended and upset. She picked up Bonzo and trailed down the garden to where the beans were coming into flower, red against the back fence.

Mummy was standing with her arms folded, talking to Major Kerr.

'. . . know she was married?' Unity heard.

'Hell, Eva, it was none of my business. Her husband's in the Pacific.'

'I don't know how she could do that.'

'She's young . . . You can't play by the rules in wartime.'

'Yes, you must, more than ever . . .'

Mummy looked round and saw her. 'Hello, my darling,' she called gaily, 'are you having a lovely time?'

'They're all indoors, or sleepy,' said Unity. She felt as if she might cry.

Mummy laughed. 'Well, we can't have that. Come on, Dan, we'll go and play a game.'

They walked back towards the house.

'You were rude,' whispered Unity anxiously.

'How was I?'

'You said Dan.'

'Oh,' Mummy laughed again. 'It's all right for grown-ups. Not for little girls.'

Colonel Robertson was standing on the lawn by himself, with the rumpled tablecloth at his feet.

'I'll have to leave now, Mrs Sherborne,' he said very politely, holding out his hand to Mummy. 'Thank you for your gracious hospitality these weeks past. This has truly been a home from home.'

Mummy took his hand, and held it. 'Oh, but we'll see you again, won't we?' she said. 'Unity will miss you. And so will I.'

'I surely don't know if that's going to be possible, ma'am.'

It dawned on Unity that he was going away for ever.

'You've got to come back! You've got to! You're my *best!*'

She hurled herself forward, sobbing, and grabbed him

round the knees. He crouched down and put his arms round her, holding her close as she wept and hiccupped into his shirt: he told her he loved her very much, too, and that she was his special sweetheart, but he didn't say he would come again. Then he went away.

'Why doesn't he want to come anymore?' she asked her mother, still crying, helping her to pick up the cushions and rugs.

'He's had a quarrel with Pat. He found out something about her that he didn't like.'

'It isn't fair for Pat to spoil everything.'

'No, it isn't,' said Mummy.

Mummy and Patricia were very polite to each other in the days that followed. Pat was often out in the evenings, but she brought no one to the house in Colonel Robertson's place.

One morning Beth came downstairs by herself. 'Patricia's not feeling so good, Mrs Sherborne,' she said. 'I guess she'd like to stay home here today.'

'That's quite all right,' said Mummy, 'but I'll be out this afternoon.'

'She knows that, ma'am,' said Beth. 'I told her myself.'

They looked at each other for a moment.

'Does she need an aspirin, or anything?'

'No, thank you, ma'am,' said Beth smiling. 'I believe she has everything she needs.'

Mummy took Unity off to the shops after dinner, calling goodbye to Pat as they left. She bustled Unity along, not talking much. At the grocer's she looked in her bag and made a tutting noise.

'Damn, I've left the ration books at home. We'll have to go back – sorry, darling.'

She walked back even faster. From the corner of the

road they could see a Jeep outside the house. Unity's heart leapt: Colonel Robertson had come back! But Mummy stopped in the street and bent down and talked to her very firmly, as if she had been naughty.

'When we get inside I want you to go straight out into the back garden and stay there until I call you. Do you understand?'

'Yes,' said Unity, 'but—'

'At once, Unity.' Mummy looked quite pale and her lips were thin.

Unity went only as far as the kitchen: she had to know if Colonel Robertson was there. She crept back to the foot of the stairs and watched her mother knock briskly on Patricia's door, push it open, and stand still in the doorway.

'Please leave,' Unity heard her say.

An officer came quickly down the stairs and out of the front door. It wasn't Colonel Robertson, it was nobody Unity had ever seen before.

Mummy still stood there. Patricia came out, in her dressing-gown.

'I think you abuse my hospitality,' said Mummy.

'Who are you to criticise, honey?' said Pat. She sounded rude.

Unity slipped quietly into the kitchen and out into the garden. Whatever it was, it was something nasty: she didn't want her mother to know that she knew about it.

When she went back, Mummy was in the kitchen. Her handbag still stood open on the table.

'You had the ration books all the time,' said Unity, looking inside.

'Good gracious, so I did. Silly me.'

Patricia left the next day, and another lady came: her

name was Sue-Ellen. Colonel Robertson started coming to see Unity again, and was just as loving as before, but things had changed. Everyone seemed to be in a hurry all the time: the men were always being called back to base or having to go off on urgent jobs, and even Colonel Robertson didn't seem to want to play as much as he had. He and the others spent a lot of time talking quietly to Mummy about Army things. Unity felt left out and got whiney and over-excited. Her mother was short-tempered with her and once or twice gave her a good slap for interrupting.

It was Unity's bedtime, but she couldn't find Bonzo. She wandered into the kitchen, where Major Kerr was helping Mummy to wash up the tea things.

'Isn't there anyone you could get to babysit?' he was asking.

'Look,' said Mummy, 'I've told you – I can't go at all.'

'Why the hell not? We're all going – a group date. What's wrong with that, Eva?'

'You don't know what it's like. All eyes – just waiting for me to put a foot wrong. I have to live in this town.'

'No you *don't*.'

'Oh don't start all that again.'

Mummy sounded upset. A knife fell to the floor. He picked it up and handed it back.

'Mind you wash it, honey.'

'Of course I'm going to wash it! What did you think I was going to do?'

'I didn't mean anything—'

'Yes you did! That's exactly what you meant! You think we're all filthy, you think Europe's filthy, you think you've all got to *rescue* us! You think you've got to rescue *me*!'

'Wow,' said the major, 'did I ever say the wrong thing.'

She gave a funny little gasping laugh and rested her head for a moment on his chest, still holding the dishcloth. He put his arms round her.

'You could use a bit of rescuing,' he said.

'How long have you been standing there, Unity?' said Mummy, pulling away from him. 'I told you to go to bed.'

'I can't find Bonzo.'

'I'll find Bonzo, and bring him up. Now do as you are told.'

Unity went upstairs and struggled into her nightie. She sat on the bed waiting for Mummy to come and wash her face and clean her teeth, but she didn't come. The voices from the kitchen sounded loud and cross; then she heard her mother running quickly up the stairs. Her bedroom door slammed.

Mummy was lying on the bed in all her clothes, with the pillow pulled over her face.

'What's the matter now?' she said from underneath.

'You didn't say goodnight,' said Unity. 'And I still haven't got Bonzo.'

'Would you be a good girl,' asked Mummy a day or two later, 'if Mrs Griffiths came to look after you on Saturday night?'

'Are you going to America?'

'To America! Of course not, that's thousands of miles away. It's just – there's a dance on at the base, and Dan – and they all want me to go. You see, they might not be here much longer. And it's ages since I went out anywhere.'

Unity thought about it. Mrs Griffiths sometimes helped Mummy out in the house. She had sticking-out teeth, but she was kind.

'All right,' she said. 'But you've got to put me to bed.'

Mummy looked beautiful the night of the dance. She'd washed her hair and waved it, and put on a blue frock she'd been saving; it fitted tight at the top and had a swirly skirt. Unity watched her put little gold rings in her ears and dab scent on her neck and temples and the front of her hair. She put some on Unity too: it smelled lovely.

'You're much prettier than Beth or Sue-Ellen,' Unity whispered.

Mummy laughed.

'I'm not bad for thirty-three.'

Unity waved them all goodbye from the window. It felt strange being in the house without Mummy: not creepy exactly, because she knew Mrs Griffiths was downstairs, but empty and a bit sad. It took a long time to get to sleep. She could hear Mrs Griffiths singing in the kitchen; later she heard Big Ben on the radio, nine o'clock. Moonlight seeped through the join of the curtains, filling the room with a pale pearly glow: she pulled the covers over her head to shut it out. She tried to imagine the dance. Mummy had said it wouldn't be anything special, not like parties before the war, but she had been excited. 'I haven't been dancing for years,' she'd said. 'Your daddy doesn't like it.'

She must have dropped off at last, because she suddenly came broad awake: it was the clicking of her mother's high heels on the pavement that had wakened her. The moonlight was much stronger now; it seemed to be

asking her to look out of the window. She knelt up on
the bed and peered cautiously through the gap in the
curtains. She could see the dark bulk of a jeep in
the road, and the garden was full of long shadows
from the trees and bushes. In the striped half-light she
couldn't see Mummy anywhere; and then she could. Eva
was standing under the cherry-tree by the front gate,
and there was someone else with her, only a dark outline,
but Unity knew it was Dan Kerr.

They were standing very close together, as they had
for that moment in the kitchen, and they were very still.
Mummy's head was against his shoulder, and his hands
must be on her waist, for the shadow of her skirt was
swaying very slightly. As she looked at them Unity felt
a great hollow place full of sadness and longing open
up inside her. She picked up Bonzo and strained him
hard against her tummy and chest.

As Unity watched, her mother lifted her head and
moved away a little. Unity could see that Dan tried to
hold her, but she put her fingers on his mouth and said
something to him; then she walked away up the path.

Unity slid quickly back into bed. She heard the jeep
start up and drive away, and her mother's key in the
lock. A little later Mrs Griffiths said goodnight in
the hall.

When her mother came in, Unity lay still as a mouse,
her eyes tight shut. Mummy rearranged the covers over
her, bent down and kissed her gently on the cheek. She
still smelled lovely.

'Goodnight, my darling love,' said Mummy softly,
and went away.

Unity gave a long sigh: her heart felt big and sore in
her chest and one or two tears came out and trickled
down her cheeks. 'Whatever are you crying for?' she

said to herself in her grown-up voice because everything surely was all right now: Mummy was back safe and the sad thing in the garden had gone away. The pain inside her eased gradually until even the crying had a sort of pleasure in it, like crying at a sad story. Unity took a deep breath through her tears and fell asleep.

In her dreams it seemed to her that her father had come home: she heard soft footsteps on the gravel and the sound of the front door opening and closing. In her dreams the house was full of murmurs and gentle noises: a man's voice, tender and soft, on the other side of her bedroom wall. In her dreams Unity knew that her mother was happy, and she floated on the wings of that happiness further and further into peaceful sleep, where even dreaming stopped.

In the morning there was just her mother and herself, and the American girls. The weather turned wet and windy, and then one day Beth and Sue-Ellen packed their things and said goodbye. Mummy shook hands with Sue-Ellen, but she hugged Beth for a long time.

When they had gone, Mummy put on an overall and tied a scarf around her hair and set about their room as if it were spring-cleaning time. Then she went on to the rest of the house, scouring and dusting and polishing. She seemed unable to sit down, and hardly let Unity out of her sight. As soon as the rain stopped she turned her restless energy to the garden, weeding her rows of young vegetables, hunting down caterpillars, putting up pea-sticks. Some of the lettuces had bolted already, and they picked the first tender runner beans and a few watery strawberries.

'I haven't been looking after this properly,' she said. 'There's a lot of catching up to do.'

'I'll help you,' said Unity, carrying a handful of weeds to the bonfire.

'You do help me, darling,' said Mummy. 'Just you and me again, now.'

'Won't they ever come back?' asked Unity sadly.

'Not until the war's over,' said Mummy, 'if at all.'

That night Unity was awakened by a roar in the sky. Wave after wave of noise was building from a distant rumble, pressing down over the roof of the little house as if to press it into the ground, and dying away only as the next wall of sound built up. She lay crushed and smothered by noise until the terror became more than she could bear.

Her mother's bed was empty. In panic, Unity began to grope her way downstairs. Halfway down she found Eva crouching in the darkness, with her head on her knees and her hands over her ears. Her small body seemed to rock with each successive wave of sound. As Unity crept to her side, Mummy put an arm out, blindly, and pulled her close: they huddled together while the monstrous force passed overhead to France.

Lost Boys

❦

Linda Leatherbarrow

'At home,' said the invitation, nothing formal. I wasn't a social animal, hated parties, but the weeks, months even, had been sliding by and I knew if I didn't go I'd only end up bitching to all and sundry about the state of my love life – non-existent state of my love life – and that would have made me a sad bastard, another sad bastard to add to the collection at work.

I work for a local authority, relocating difficult children from school to special unit then back again to school. It may sound like *Catcher In the Rye* but it isn't really. You fall into stuff and that's how it was with me, the Job Centre sending me for an interview and me thinking No Danger, then getting taken on. Local authorities are repositories for all the saddos.

However, it wasn't work I was thinking about that morning. I stood in front of the long cupboard in my bedroom like a murderer staring into a drain through which had passed the boiled and strained remains of a decade's corpses, a murderer who can't imagine how he came to be like this, no longer remembers when it started and can't imagine when it will end. But, before you skip on to something more cheerful, bear in mind that I only said *like*. *Like* a murderer. It was just a feeling.

Inside my cupboard were hundreds of white cardboard shoe boxes and I was tempted to take one down, open it up, check that the contents were still as I remembered, but the secret of successful design, whatever you may hear to the contrary, the *real* secret is no self-referral, no retrospection, no nostalgia. Each shoe was a one-off, worn for one night and one night only. Hence the feeling.

Rabbit shoes, fruit basket shoes, rhino shoes with horns, cavalier, cowboy, sharks, even bed of nail shoes. I rummaged through my fabric box, pulling out tassels and Chinese patterned silks, snake skin, pony skin, half-heartedly debating the possibilities of postage stamps, even padlocks, but decided, after a day of it, that fetish was better left to Vivienne Westwood. I didn't go to art school all those years just to do platforms. Ah, I hear you say, what's he doing working for a local authority if he trained to be an artist? And this is where I put you straight. Virtually everyone employed by a local authority is trained to do something else. That's what I meant about repositories.

The radio bleated from a shelf. Apparently it was St David's Day.

On St David's Day, my grandmother, my Welsh grandmother, Blodwin Anastasia Todd (they had proper names in those days), always wore a daffodil in her buttonhole, never once forgot. It might have been spring but it wasn't a daffodil spring. Cold enough for snow. Forget daffs – too Mother's Day, too Easter Bunny. But Blodwin winked at me from her grave on the side of a bare Welsh hill and, in a flurry of inspiration, I sketched a design in the margin of a library book. I have no compunction about drawing in margins or adding notes, or inscriptions for that matter. Reading an annotated book is as good as holding hands.

I hunted through various greengrocers for the largest leeks with the longest roots. They had to be fresh and firm. They had to be deep Hooker's green on the outside, sweet yellow lime on the inside, a fat white stump at the base. I bought four to allow for prototypes (past experience says that you never, ever succeed the first time) then hunted for the right base shoes, size nine stilettos, any colour. Tried Oxfam, tried Romanian Orphans and was finally successful in Cancer Relief. They were even comfortable.

I walked them up and down while the ladies behind the counter smirked. Of course I played up to them. Who wouldn't? I can do theatrical, I can do camp, though I'd rather not do eccentric. Tucked away beneath my clean boy image, the crisp white shirt, grey flannels, my poor mad mother stares at the telly, in love with a newscaster, and Blodwin is coming through the back door to rescue me, though it felt more like kidnapping at the time. If only they knew, I thought, but I wasn't being fair. Both ladies had a distinctly In-Love-with-a-Newscaster look themselves. They had glazed eyes, fragile hair and they smelt like Mother – dried roses and Vaseline Intensive Care.

Back home, I sliced the first leek lengthwise to within an inch of its base, cut out the heart, then slipped the left shoe between the leaves, pushed the pointed toe down into the stump, glued the outer leaves along the sides. Superglue is wonderful stuff. I over-lapped and bunched the leaves at the back. It was tricky but a little perseverance and I had it: then I sheared off the leaves with my sharp cook's knife, wrapped a pale inside leaf up the heel, let it fan out a little at the back. I was careful to arrange the leaves at different angles, to lay the dark against the light until the shoe appeared to be made entirely from vegetable, a bulb-toed pump with a curly root flourish.

Sitting down, I tried it on, crossed my legs, let it swing in the air. Perfect. I got up and put Etta James on and, while she was giving her all, 'I'd rather go blind' and 'Don't pick me for a fool', I made another to match, varnished them both, then knocked up a quiche with the remaining leeks and two eggs. I didn't have any cream. Which annoyed me.

The following evening, I ran the clippers over my hair, put on my grey Italian suit, my best suit, sixties mohair, newly back from the cleaner's. For a few hours, I'd be sharp as a razor blade. That was the theory. I slipped into a pair of white silk socks, yes, I know – Essex boy, but no other colour would have worked with the leeks, then I put on the shoes and stared into the mirror.

I wasn't young anymore but I wasn't old. The mirror confirmed this. Neither one thing nor the other, in between, neither charmingly innocent, nor innocently charming.

All this effort and now, predictably, I was down. Call it stage fright, call it what you like; it makes no difference. Everything had to be perfect; everything *was* perfect. Except for my ears – huge, jutting, pinkly translucent, snail trails of light on the rims. And why did I only have one eyebrow, joined in the middle like a transmogrifying werewolf? I turned the mirror to the magnifying side, plucked out the hairs with my tweezers until the space between my brows was an angry pink. I couldn't possibly go. Even as I decided this, I picked up the phone and called a mini-cab.

Purse, spectacles, keys. The spectacles are five years

old with round goofy lenses. I don't really need them, yet, if I go out without them, some dip-stick is bound to wave a British Rail timetable at me, or a phone book, never a book of love poems or photographs of interesting people looking fabulous. It took forever to find the keys, turning over the heaps and welter, the underside of previous creations, snippets of pink suede, drifts of feathers. When I was at school the teacher used to say, 'Nigel, a tidy desk is a tidy mind.' I never understood the advantage of a tidy mind. All the same, I couldn't help wondering why I didn't have a special place for my keys, a brass plate on a whatnot in the hall. Maybe when I'm forty . . .

When the cab came, I sat in the back; there's nothing like inhaling the musk of other people's dreams, watching the city reel by. London is the best city in the world and I should know because I've lived here all my adult life, have never lived in another city, unless you count Birmingham and that, well, frankly, that isn't a city any more than McDonald's is a restaurant.

Birmingham was where I took my degree, where I made my first pair of shoes – crocodiles with real teeth from a shop behind New Street Station, second-hand teeth that leered at me from green baize plinths in the window, drawing me in. I had to have them. The next morning I woke with someone else's stomach curled against my back, someone else's arm heavy over my ribs.

It wasn't a reassuring door – a battered hulk, driftwood peeled from a shoreline, traces of paint clinging like salt. Behind me, the alleyway faded into the dark and, above me, there were balconies, hooks, relics, mysterious chunks of rusty metal embedded in brick, horrible dangerous things that could have dropped down on my head at any second. Maybe they wouldn't open the door. It was the wrong night, or the wrong door. Maybe, just maybe, there would be someone I hadn't met before – a possible. I was sweaty-palmed, dry-mouthed, all the usual symptoms. I should have taken a Valium. Get on with it, I thought. Ring the bell.

'Come in, come in, thought you weren't going to make it.'

'So did I.'

'Yeah?'

'Trains,' I said vaguely then sprung up the metal stairs behind my host, the leeks going up as if they'd dedicated their life to climbing stairs.

I wondered if they'd know how to come down, if the root toes would trip me up, if I'd have to turn and lower myself backwards on all fours like my sister's baby, Aimee, ten months, who just that week had learned to go upstairs and then down, Aimee who held up her arms and crinkled her eyes in a smile that I believed was especially for me even though it was more logical to suppose she was only practising and smiled like that at everyone.

When we went in, I saw at once that the room was full of rich bastards or people who spent their lives making people richer than them even richer – total schmucks. Couldn't imagine why I'd been invited. I edged into a room full of flat-edged smiles, slip-streamed myself into the shoal. Big fish, little fish. I could always get loaded, I thought. Later, if all else fails.

'Darling!'

'Lovely to see you.'

'Darling, your shoes! How fabulous! Look everyone – Nigel's feet. Why haven't you got a shop, darling?

Somewhere delicious where we can come and buy delicious things?'

Obviously the leeks were a mistake. I gave a little wave, pretending to spot someone I knew, clumped across the room, and buried myself in a suitably bucolic corner, flowerpots with grasses, the sort of thing that suggests a pent and suicidal moggy who, in between running up curtains and shredding wallpaper, chokes down dusty blades and stalks in the hope of making itself sick, a cat that is never allowed out. After a bit the grass triggered off the hay fever so I had to decamp, this time opting for a sky-blue leather sofa next to a table covered with huge glass bowls brimming with raspberries, strawberries and blood-red sangria. I spooned down some raspberries and began to cheer up. Was there, could there be in all this smooth-jowled agitation, a possible?

It was late but no one seemed to be drinking – the kind of party where everyone has a breakfast meeting in a few hours time and can't afford to drink. Filling a glass, I sat back, swung one leg over the other, let the sangria seep into my brain. The toes of my shoes were bluntly, sweetly fleshy. I am yours, I thought, to no one in particular.

I had another glass, and another, then there by the window I saw someone and between us the smiles darted, the current flowed, and I put up my hand, stroked my cat's fur scalp, rubbed it the wrong way. It was a long time since anyone other than Aimee had rubbed my fur, the wrong way or *any* way. Uncrossing my legs, I stretched them out, pointed the shoes directly across the room, smiled a long slow smile: I am not a little fish, I am your little fish.

'What wonderful shoes.'

'Yes,' I said. 'I like a little frivolity at the feet.'

When I got home the next day, it smelt like a tenement out of *1984*, cabbage soup, dirty underwear, but it was only the leek trimmings, wilting in a trapezoid of sunlight on the floor. My shoes were pinching my toes. Taking them off, I carried them barefoot across the room. The white socks were still under his sheets at the foot of a bed I hadn't cared to explore, not since the time I'd encountered a slimy knuckle bone buried by *that* possible's dog, a border collie with a tongue it couldn't keep to itself.

I opened my cupboard and looked at the boxes, remembering the smell of wet hair after a shower, a birthmark the size of a rose petal pressed onto an upturned buttock, remembering...well, remembering too many details. The process of seduction these days is like doing a job interview, each of you explaining the intricacies of jobs neither of you is interested in. Leek Shoes worked in the Westminster Reference Library, not that I let that faze me. As I said, it had been weeks, even months, besides it gave us something in common. One local government officer to another even helped speed things along.

Reaching up, I opened an empty box, dropped in the shoes then sat down on the bed. If I find myself sinking, it's a habit of mine to think about a polar bear. The bear dances on sheets of ice, pirouettes, graceful, powerful. Sometimes the bear skates on two legs, head up, front legs held clasped behind its back. Sometimes it glides on one leg. That day, it reminded me of school.

We used to slide on a strip of ice that formed each year in the yard, at the corner of the kitchen block, where the guttering dripped, used to stand in a long line waiting our turn. Strangely, the big boys didn't always go first, ice making them charitable, the little boys venturing out with wing-stick arms as if the air could catch them. Where were they now? No doubt leading useful lives but lost – lost to me. Here the bear returned, plodding in a tartan overcoat on all fours like a manicured poodle taken for a walk, trudging over white snow under a white sky. After a bit, all I could see was the tartan coat.

I changed into jeans and trainers, caught the tube to Oxford Circus and John Lewis and, for once, went straight past Haberdashery. In the children's department, I bought a pair of gold kid slippers with tee-bar straps, tiny gold buttons, the neatest buttonholes. I undid them then did them up again – neither too tight, nor too loose. They sat on the palm of my hand and I stroked them with my thumb, the softest leather you could buy. Made in Italy. Size One.

'Gift wrapped,' I told the assistant then wrote on the card: To Aimee with love. Big kiss.

Outside, Oxford Street was dark with impending rain. Men and boys floated by, dangerous animals. I watched their shoulder blades beneath their jackets, long legs cutting through the tide. For some reason, I thought of Blodwin sending me off in the mornings, smoothing down my hair. Fourteen and her still tucking in my tie. 'Beautiful you are,' she said. 'Break their hearts, laddo, break a leg.' Used to make me cringe.

When I got home, there was a message on the answerphone.

'Thanks for a lovely time. See you tonight. Dinner at Yamina's. I'll pick you up at eight.'

Yamina's was the new Moroccan on the corner. I'd been meaning to try it. What I couldn't figure out was how he'd got my number and how he knew where I lived. I played his message over again, then again. He had a deep voice, a warm smiling kind of voice and I had the strangest feeling I'd been thrown a line and it would be churlish to throw it back. Stupid even. Etta James was still on the player so I pressed the Play button, 'Only time will tell', then opened my cupboard and looked at the boxes.

Several years ago, I'd made a pair of yellow Moroccan mules with silk embroidery and curled up toes. It took me a few moments to locate them.

Goin' Dancin'

Rowena Macdonald

'**S**o, Rena, you got a boyfriend?' asked Carole, as we sat folding napkins into pointy hats.

'No, not really,' I said. I didn't bother to correct her over my name.

'No! Pretty girl like you. I don't believe it.' The brittle way she said this sounded as if she believed it completely – but then everything Carole said had an underlying note of bitchiness. She knocked another menthol cigarette from her packet and lit up, regarding me through the smoke with a glint in her small brown eyes. It was a look I had seen before. Sometimes I would glance up from serving a table and find her eyes on me as if she was plotting something.

'Well, you and me should go out together sometime. Find ourselves boyfriends. What you doin' on your days off?'

'Going to Toronto.'

'Toronto! Goin' to Toronto? Hear that, boss, Rena's goin' to Toronto.' Alex, our boss, carried on staring up the street and punching one fist into the palm of his other hand.

'Haven't you ever been to Toronto?' I asked Carole.

'Me? No, I ain't even been out of Quebec.'

*

Once everyone had gone we vacuumed under the tables and brushed the dead fruit flies from the placemats. We wiped the crumbs from the chair seats and polished the rubber plants with milk. The restaurant was fitted out in pastel colours – beige carpet, apricot tablecloths, mint green walls – neither downmarket nor sophisticated, merely bland. The only hints that it was a Greek restaurant were a badly painted mural of some unidentified Greek gods and a shelf of empty Metaxa bottles. We dusted the bottles and the 'horizontal surfaces', according to Alex's instructions, and laid the tables for the following day, Carole placing the knives with the cutting edge outwards and me facing them inwards.

'Hey, Rita, you're doin' the knives wrong. You gotta face them this way,' she shouted.

'That's not the way I was taught to lay a table.'

'Well, this is the right way, sweetie. It's more friendly to have the knives like this. More welcoming.'

Saturday breakfast was my next shift. Breakfasts were a new venture for Alex and he had hung a yellow plastic banner over the front of the restaurant, which read: CALIFORNIA STYLE BREAKFASTS SERVED HERE.

'Boss said we gotta wipe down the *terrasse*, sweetie,' said Carole. This was my least favourite job. It involved wiping all the dust, ketchup and spilt sugar off the plastic *terrasse* furniture.

A strange heightened light bathed the street and the lime trees rustled ominously in the breeze. A cacophony of barking resounded from the pet shop next door. The shop was holding a charity pet auction and there were several dogs in cages out on the forecourt.

'Ain't he cute?' said Carole, leaning over the fence to gaze at a rottweiler that was trying to chew through the wire of its cage. 'He's just too adorable. Shame I ain't got enough room in my apartment for him. We used to have a rottweiler when I was a kid . . . Eh, Rena, we used to have a rottweiler.'

'Oh yeah?' I carried on wiping. A smartly-dressed couple walked past and stood hand in hand looking at the menu board.

'Excuse me. Do you do breakfasts?' asked the man. I could tell by his thin whiney voice that he would be a bad tipper.

'Yep, we do, sir,' said Carole, pointing towards the sign.

'What's a California-style breakfast?' asked the woman, wrinkling her nose as if she suspected it might not be very nice.

'It's basically the same as a Canadian breakfast except it has fruit on the plate. All the plates have fruit,' I replied.

'Fruit. Okay. Can I just ask you something? Do you do egg-white omelettes?'

'I'm not sure. I'd have to ask the chef . . .'

'Course we do, sweetie. Egg-white omelette – no problem,' interrupted Carole.

'Well, maybe we'll come back tomorrow.' We watched them cross the road and inspect the flowers outside the Chinese supermarket on the corner. Garish carnations were on special offer at two dollars a bunch.

'Always tell 'em what they wanna hear, sweetie – you unnerstand? . . . So anyway I was tellin' you about our rottweiler, wasn't I? Called Sugar, he was – you know after Sugar Ray Robinson, that boxer. I wanted to call him Mohammed after Mohammed Ali but Daddy said it was a stupid name. Anyway it was really tragic 'cos Daddy had to shoot Sugar in the end . . .'

A spot of water dropped on my arm. Within seconds rain was hammering down like a monsoon. We had to grab the salt and pepper shakers off the freshly-wiped tables and dash inside.

'Fucking weather. And those fucking dogs are driving me nuts,' said Alex. He strode through the restaurant, his brow furrowed furiously, 'Gimme a beer.'

I fetched a Molson from the fridge. He took it into the bathroom, muttering that he had to 'take a slash'.

The rain poured all morning. When it stopped the air steamed in the humid heat and rainbow puddles of petrol shimmered on the road.

During a lull Carole and I shared a cold Kraft cheese omelette, sent back by a customer who had wanted feta cheese.

'You eat the rest, sweetie, I'm dietin',' said Carole, pushing her ketchup-drenched half towards me. 'Hey, I never finished tellin' you 'bout Sugar, did I?'

'Oh yeah, why did your dad shoot him?'

'Well, he bit my brother Roger. So Daddy said he had to be put down – the dog, that is. Roger'd been foolin' around trying to dress him in a frock and make him walk on his hind legs and Sugar just bit his little finger right off. Roger's been scared of dogs ever since. Crosses the street if he sees a dog coming along – even if it's on a lead . . .' Course, he *is* the sensitive type.'

She gave a knowing nod, angling for me to ask her why Roger was 'the sensitive type'.

'Why is Roger the sensitive type?'

'He's a little bit, you know . . .' She flapped her wrist. 'He's a gay. I mean he got married and all – he tried. But we all knew he was a gay right from when he was a kid. You know, Rena, he was like a mother to me. 'Cos my mother, she worked so hard – always out working. So he took care of us. Did all the cleanin', all the cookin' – boy, could he cook! And cakes! He was the best cake baker ever . . . his chocolate mayonnaise cake . . . mmm – to die for.' She raised her eyes to heaven. 'And you know what, Rena? He used to wear red pants. Well! It was obvious – we all knew – I mean, boys just didn't wear red pants in those days. And he used to wear his shirt tied – at the front, like a girl. Oh, it was obvious . . .'

She laughed and the laughter turned into a coughing fit until she had to thump her chest with her fist.

'We used to go out dancin' together – oh, he was *such* a good dancer. And we always ended up chasin' after the same boys. It was so funny. Hey, *we* better not start chasin' the same fellas, eh Rena?'

'When?'

'When we go out dancin'.'

'Oh, right.'

After we had polished the cutlery with vinegar and cashed up, I took off my waitressing shoes and slipped on my flip-flops.

'I just wanna say something to you, sweetie,' said Carole, leaning in close enough for me to see a few dark hairs that she'd missed on her chin.

'Yes?'

'Well, Alex asked me to tell you that you really oughta wear a skirt. The customers like it, see. It's better for you too – you get better tips.'

'Why couldn't Alex tell me himself?'

'He felt it was better coming from me, sweetie. You know, 'cos I'm your friend.'

I bought a cheap skirt from Le Chateau, which Carole

pronounced to be 'cute, but a little long'. 'Really you want something that shows off your legs, sweetie. Like *my* skirt. You get beautiful tips that way.'

Carole's skirt finished halfway up her thighs. Her legs were hard from thirty years running around restaurants. They didn't match the soft lumpiness of her upper body.

Alex had brought in a new waitress for a trial. He stood behind her, grinning broadly, and said, 'Ladies, this is Suzi. Show her the ropes. Okay?'

Suzi was tall and blond with heavy make-up and glasses that magnified her eyes enormously. She drifted between the tables with her back held very straight, her high heels clicking loudly on the floor.

''Ow can I 'elp you? Do you need any 'elp?,' she repeated plaintively in a high-pitched Quebec accent, beseeching us with her huge eyes. We showed her how to fold napkins but she couldn't get the hang of it and kept having to stop for a cigarette break.

'You waitressed much before, sweetie?' Carole asked her, as we ate souvlakis at the end of the shift. Suzi had refused food and was retouching her make-up with great concentration in the mirror behind the bar.

'Of course. I was cocktail waitress in Miami. In a big 'otel. I didn't like it. And before that I was waitress at the Copacobana.'

'Oh yeah – the Copacobana. I know it.'

'I was there when it first open. It was the first club in Montreal to 'ave dancers, you know, wearing nothing 'ere.' She pointed to her breasts. 'Not me, of course – I keep my clothes on. We 'ad all the shows from Las Vegas. We 'ad to wear short skirts and fishnets. Fifty dollar tips we get – you know, for looking at your legs.'

''Course I used to work in a go-go bar too,' said Carole. 'Go-go girls on one side and me behind the bar.

Used to make myself these little costumes – you know, with the fringin' and all. And you know what? – I used to make more money than the go-go girls. Can you believe that?'

'Which bar?' asked Suzi.

'The Golden Nugget down on Réné Lévesque. It ain't there no more. Country and western bar it was. Me, I worked every kind of place – bars, casinos, hotels, restaurants. Been workin' since I was thirteen.'

'Thirteen! Didn't you go to school?' I asked.

'I couldn't, sweetie! I mean I was smart at school. Top of the class. But my daddy left and Mom couldn't afford to bring us all up on her own. Seven of us there were. Used to give her all my wages I did.'

'Seven kids!'

'Yep. Typical Quebeckers my mom and dad. All they did was drink and make babies. Ain't that right, Suzi? Typical Quebeckers.' She cackled raucously, hacked and thumped her chest, then spat into a napkin, 'Excuse me, ladies.'

'You okay, Carole?' I asked.

'Yep, sweetie.' After hawking into the napkin again she said, 'Tomorrow I'm gettin' a patch. I can't take this no more.' She lit another menthol cigarette and inhaled so hard her cheeks caved in.

'I 'ave to call my boyfriend,' said Suzi.

'So when we gonna go out and find ourselves boyfriends?' said Carole, when Suzi had disappeared to use the phone.

'I don't know.'

'Soon as we get paid let's go out dancin'. How 'bout that? You up for that, Rhianne?'

'You mean – go out tonight?'

'Yeah, why not? No time like the present, eh Rena?'

'Right Carole.'

It was supposed to be our pay day so I went to find Alex. He was in his windowless office, slowly tapping numbers into a calculator. As soon as I appeared he swivelled in his chair and leant back, barring my entry with his feet on the doorframe. For the first time ever I was relieved when he said we would have to wait a few more days for our pay.

'Guess we'll have to go dancin' another day,' said Carole, when I told her the bad news.

'Guess so,' I said.

I noticed her staring intently at my legs. 'You wearin' nylons, Rena?'

'No, it's too hot for tights.'

'You gotta wear nylons.'

'Why?'

'It's against the law not to, sweetie. Unhygienic. Diners don't wanna be eatin' their food with your bare legs in their face.'

Suzi nodded, 'I think Carole is correct.'

'I really hate wearing tights,' I said.

'You think I like wearin' nylons in this heat?' said Carole, 'You gotta wear 'em. Alex won't like it if he finds out you ain't wearin' nylons.'

Suzi wasn't asked back after her trial. 'Something was badly wrong in her brain. She was a little complexed,' said Alex, twisting his forefinger into his temple.

The following day I was cutting jello into one-inch squares when a red-haired woman walked in. I jumped up and moved towards her with a menu.

'Hey Rita, how ya doin'?' shouted the woman.

'Carole! I didn't recognise you. New hair.'

'You like it?' Carole twirled, patting her newly-dyed

hair. She had gone from frizzy bleached blonde to sleek bright mahogany. 'I did it myself. I used to be a hairdresser, you know.'

'Very nice.'

'I thought I'd better do my hair if we're goin' out dancin'.'

'Are we?'

'I thought we agreed. You ain't backin' out on me now, are you, Rena?'

'I thought we were going to wait 'til pay day.'

'You mean you don't wanna go?'

'No, it's just that I don't have any money.'

Carole marched behind the counter and began to change from her high-heeled mules into flat lace-ups. She fumbled in her handbag for her cigarettes and lit up. I noticed she had outlined her lips in dark red to make them look bigger. She poured a coffee from the jug that had been standing on the hot ring all morning and switched the radio to Oldies 990.

'I got some nylons, Carole,' I said, holding up a leg for her to inspect. Carole nodded curtly and began to tidy along the counter in a brisk, irritable way.

As the day wore on she brightened up, wiggling her way through the tables with five plates on one arm and singing along to Diana Ross in a Tammy Wynette voice.

'Pretty good singer, ain't I?' she declared. The old Jewish ladies picking at their fillets of sole smiled indulgently.

When Elvis came on singing 'Hound Dog' she grabbed my hand behind the dirty dishes screen and showed me how to rock and roll. Ravi and Spiros, the chefs, laughed at us through the serving hatch.

'Not a bad dancer, eh Rita? Yep, Carole, she knows how to have a good time.'

Alex burst through the kitchen doors as if he was entering a cowboy bar. 'Enough fooling around. You got clients.' Alex always referred to the diners as clients.

'We're just havin' a giggle, boss. Customers like to see a happy waitress,' said Carole, sashaying off towards her section.

Alex stood at the window rubbing his stomach, which was beginning to flop over his jeans. A boy in a red shirt with grass-coloured hair walked past.

'Hey, check out the green hair,' said Alex. He turned to me, 'What you think of green hair . . . you find it attractive?'

'Not particularly.'

'I think it's sick. You know what these people are? They're very complexed. You know what it is they're doing? – it's trying to make a statement, that's what it is. Sick!'

Disgusted, he marched out towards the Chinese supermarket, where he liked to sit with the owner drinking beer and watching TV when the restaurant was quiet.

I tried to avoid Carole by keeping to my section in case she mentioned going out dancing again. Nobody came in for a long while so I slumped against the wall and stared vacantly out of the window. The sun beat down and a kind of deadness hung over the *terrasse* and the empty tree-lined street. 'Penny Lane' came on the radio and I suddenly felt homesick. I wondered what I was doing so far away from England, working with a woman who didn't even know my proper name.

'If you were gettin' paid for smiles, you'd be very poor,' said Carole. 'Customers like to see happy waitresses. It adds to the ambulance . . .'

'The what?'

'You know, the ambulance.'

*

Spiros sat with us when lunch was over. He chewed a match between his teeth and let Carole smoke his cigarettes.

'Like my hair, Spiros?' she demanded.

'Beautiful. Sexy lady. How you get it go so flat?' asked Spiros.

'Oh I just blow-dried it and lacquered it. Just gotta hope it don't rain else it'll go all frizzy again. I gotta blow-dry it every day to keep it like this.'

She looked at me with her head on one side and said, 'I could do so much with your hair, Rena. You really oughta get it styled.'

'I'm growing it out.'

'Yeah, but it has no shape, sweetie. It has no style. What you would suit is a short style with maybe some blond highlights. Highlights would look beautiful. Make you look like Lady Di. What you think, Spiros? Don't you think she'd look like Lady Di?'

'Lady Di. Sexy lady,' said Spiros.

'You know what you should do, sweetie? Come round to my apartment and I'll do your hair and then we should go out dancin'. Whaddya say?' Carole nodded encouragingly.

'I don't know. Maybe.'

'Me and Rena're gonna go out and find ourselves boyfriends. Gonna get some sexercise. Ain't we, Rena, eh?' She cackled and started coughing and thumping her chest.

'Did you get a patch?' I asked.

'Not yet. I gotta get one. My doctor said I gotta quit 'cos I got sixteen cysts on my breasts. One of them's cancerous, he thinks.' She took a deep drag on her cigarette and turned towards the wall as if her eyes were welling up with tears. None of us knew what to say but at least it had got her off the subject of dancing.

The next day we were paid. Carole kept rushing to the bathroom, hissing loudly in my ear that she was 'bleedin''.

'God I'm bleedin' real bad, Reenie. It's soaked right through my panties,' she informed me, as we stood scraping unfinished moussaka into the bin.

A couple of men came in and ordered filet mignons, stressing the French words in a camp over-exaggerated way.

'Some kind of faggots over there,' muttered Alex darkly, leaning in to my ear as if he was letting me in on a great secret, 'Not that I got anything against faggots . . .'

'No, live and let live,' I replied.

'Exactly. Live and let live. That's the best thing you could have said . . . Are you a lesbian or something?'

'No.'

'Just the way you said that, I thought, maybe, you know, you were a lesbian.'

He pushed past me behind the counter and ran himself a pint of water. After downing it in one and wiping his mouth with his hand, he told me at length about a lesbian strip show he'd once seen on Ste Catherine.

' . . . The two girls, let me tell you – they were knockouts. And I tell you something else – that show will stick with me for the rest of my life. Wooh, there's some things you see that you don't forget in a hurry . . .' He rubbed his stomach and slammed back through the kitchen doors, pushing his beer belly before him.

Later a black guy came in and ordered pizza. He was excessively polite when I took his order and showered me with gratitude when his pizza arrived. From the corner of my eye I could see Carole leaning against the counter, chewing her lip and watching me.

'Rena, can I say a little thing to you, sweetie?' she said as I walked past.

'Yep?'

'You shoulda cut a slice and put it on his plate for him.'

'Why?'

'It's what you do when you're servin' pizza. It adds a little bit of class, sweetie, you unnerstand?'

'Nobody has ever done that for me when I've eaten pizza,' I said.

'Well, they don't do it at Pizzahut, sweetie, but in a classy place like this, that's what you do. It looks nice. Presentation, you know what I mean?'

She sauntered off, humming a Shania Twain tune and I went behind the counter to fold a few more napkins. Alex burst through the kitchen doors, demanded a Molson and wandered over to have a chat with the black guy.

'Think you got an admirer there,' he said after the guy had left. 'You wanna know what he said?'

'What?'

'We were talking about women and he said he was looking for a woman that's not too thin but, you know – a good size – and then he said, "Like your waitress over there." '

'Sure he weren't talkin' about me?' said Carole, swishing past with a tray above her head, 'Lot of these young guys, they really go for me, you know? Sometimes I go out dancin' with my son and I get all these young guys comin' over. They like an older woman, see. For the experience, you know? They like the fact that I'm experienced.'

'Sure, Carole, whatever you say,' said Alex, rolling his eyes behind her back. He swigged his beer and turned to me, 'So whaddya say? You want me to fix you up with him? He lives up the road. Nice guy. I known him a while.'

'Me and Rena can find our own boyfriends. We don't need to be fixed up. Ain't that right, Rena? Fact we're goin' out tonight, now we've been paid. Goin' out dancin'. Right Rena?'

'Right Carole,' I said weakly.

'Carole, I think one of your clients is calling you,' said Alex, barging back into the kitchen.

At the end of the shift we sat cashing up. I had to use a calculator but Carole added up her takings on the back of her order pad, filling it with long sloping numbers. She left a cigarette burning in the ashtray as she scribbled and the smoke drifted into my eyes.

'So where we gonna meet then?' she asked, licking the seal on the takings envelope with one swipe of her tongue.

'I don't know. You choose.'

'How about La Cabane on St Laurent? It's right near Ballattou – you know, that reggae club. We can have a few drinks, then head on up to Ballattou. Seein' as you're so hot on black guys.'

'Okay. La Cabane,' I said, rubbing my eyes. 'How are you feeling? You know . . .' I indicated my head in the direction of her groin.

'Oh, it's fine now. I'm still bleedin'. But I ain't gonna let that stop me goin' out dancin'. Can't let your periods rule your life, eh Rhianne?'

*

La Cabane was almost empty so I sat at the bar to feel less conspicuous and ordered a gin and tonic. I had changed out of my white shirt and black skirt into a pink shirt and blue jeans. My toenails were freshly painted red and looked good against my white mules. The effect was only slightly spoilt by the plasters stuck to the blisters on my heels. I ran a few conversation topics through my head – though it was unlikely, knowing Carole, that there would be any awkward silences between us.

The bar began to fill up but there was no sign of her. I kept checking the door ostentatiously to make sure it was obvious I was waiting for someone and not just drinking alone.

After three gin and tonics I left. At home I lay in bed listening to the fireworks bursting over La Ronde and wished I had someone to go and watch them with. I felt surprisingly drunk and had to keep one foot on the floor to stop the room from spinning.

I never saw Carole again. The next day she didn't turn up for work. Or the next day, or the next.

'She ain't no loss. Plenty of other waitresses be queuing up to work here,' said Alex.

Generation

Louise Doughty

When the Mongol hoardes finally broke the siege of Kiev, they found themselves in something of a quandary. The Prince of Kiev was a coward. Instead of coming out to die on the castle battlements alongside the remnants of his retinue, he ran to find his ancient wet-nurse, Elka, and buried his face in her skirts.

Elka was not amused. At seventy years of age, she had every hope of dying peacefully in her bed (supine on a fat heap of cushions, surrounded by candles). She had earned it. Fifty years of looking after spoiled princelings had taken its toll.

'Save me Dearest Mother!' the Prince of Kiev cried, his voice muffled through the handfuls of dirndl skirt which he had stuffed into his mouth.

'I'm not your Dearest Mother,' Elka replied irritably. 'My name is Elka Chubukshiyeva, Nurse, and I brought you up to go out and die like a man.'

The Prince of Kiev raised his face. 'But they are *Tatars*,' he gasped. 'They will cut me open and show me my own heart while it is still beating, they will pour burning oil down my throat, they will skin me alive.' It was true that the Mongols did have a terrible reputation.

Elka rose and pushed the Prince off her lap, a task she performed with ease as she was a huge woman, her bulk undiminished by age, and her master reduced to a limp heap by his terror.

'Prince Mykhailo, Prince of Princes!' she declared in her most ringing tones. 'For generations this city has been the toast of Europe. We have had more merchants through our gates than Constantinople. We're halfway down a bloody great river that takes a trading ship all the way to the Greeks. And all you princes have done is fight amongst yourselves. What do you think it's been like for the rest of us?' She paused to look down and brush at the folds of her skirt. 'Maybe a touch of Mongol discipline is just what this dynasty needs.'

From outside the castle there came a huge roar, a mixture of triumph and dismay. The Mongols had broken through the castle walls. Soon, they would be at the main door. Once they had slaughtered the maids in the royal apartments, they would begin to scour the rest of the rooms. Elka had her own quarters at the top of the east wing, up a narrow circular staircase, but it was only a matter of time.

Elka sat down again and sighed. She hoped that their swords were sharp and would dispatch her swiftly. Surely she was too old to be messed around with. Even Tatars had mothers, after all.

The Prince was sobbing now, still kneeling at her feet. Out of pity, she drew his head back onto her lap and stroked his thinning brown hair.

I have loved this head, she thought. This head rested upon my knee when the hair on it was full and soft as the feathers at a bird's throat. I nursed this boy 'til he was four. I knew even then he would be a hopeless prince. He was always a weakling. He should never have grown up.

The Prince became quieter and turned his head so

that she could rub his temples with the balls of her fingers, the way she had when he was small. They had not sat together this way for thirty years.

Elka lifted her head and gazed out of the window at the tiny rectangle of white sky, framed in stone. It had been such a terrible winter that the window had been shuttered for months. Elka had instructed her maid to open it only once, when the straw on the floor had become infested with mice and needed sweeping out. The frozen light had been shocking after so many weeks of candlelight.

The window was open again now. Elka had pushed back the stiff shutters just before the Prince had appeared in her doorway. She had every intention of watching the sky while she waited to die. She would never see it again, after all. It was interesting to observe the sky reduced.

The Prince in her lap prevented her from rising and mounting a stool to peer out of the window and view the battle below but Elka did not need to see it. The sounds were enough. The Mongols were dispatching the last of the Royal Guard at the main door. Soon, they would gain the Great Hall. The cries were from the battlements at present, but they would quickly acquire the echoey quality of shouts from inside the building. The end would be approaching rapidly, then.

She listened to the sounds: the rising, falling tide of human wails, an orchestra of carnage punctuated now and then by a holler of triumph. It was an interesting noise, innately paradoxical. Grief and victory – those inseparable twins.

'It is all ending,' she thought, 'the glories of Kiev. Ah well, I'm glad to have seen it. I've been lucky.' The women in her family had all been wet-nurses to noblemen, the only profession where a woman was fed well and allowed to produce as many daughters as she liked. Family legend had it that a distant ancestor had been nurse to Jaroslav the Wise and lived to see him lay the first stone of the Church of Saint Sophia. Elka had had two daughters of her own, Sade and Alha, both nurses, both dead now.

Elka had outlived almost everyone she loved, bar the hopeless Prince and her elder daughter's daughter Mina, now maid to a spice merchant in Podil, the trading quarter. Mina was thirty years old, but still beautiful. Elka wondered what was happening to her.

Elka closed her eyes, the balls of her fingers still rubbing at the Prince's temples, as much for her own comfort as his. Dear God in Heaven, she thought, Mighty One. I know that the Prince and I will die, and soon. I will be killed quickly perhaps – the Prince, only you know how. But Dear Lord, please spare my little Mina, even though she is not little anymore. She has always been a fine girl, good to her old grandmother. She is worthy of saving, O Great One, although this useless bag of bones in my lap is not. For myself, well you know, I am long overdue to rest in your embrace.

And so the Mongols found them, less than an hour later. They had not moved. The Prince had his nurse's skirts pulled up around his ears against the noise of war and his cheeks sandwiched between her thighs against the certain knowledge of his certain end. The nurse had her eyes closed and her face lifted, as if to offer up her plump neck to a speedy dispatch.

The first Tatar through the door was Weg, a brute, who took her at her word and cut her throat with one swift gesture of his sabre, which was mercifully sharp.

He might have done the same for the Prince, having failed to recognise the kneeling man, had Batu Khan himself not stepped through the narrow doorway just in time and cried, 'Stop! It is he!'

Weg turned, his sabre lifted, the Prince dangling from his grasp. 'What, *him*?'

Weg dropped Prince Mykhailo on the stone floor, threw back his head and roared with laughter.

Therein lay the nature of the Mongols' quandary. It was against the rules to kill a sovereign unless in battle. If the Prince had lifted a dagger to Weg, or even turned in his grasp, then Batu could have ordered him to be run through on the spot. But an honest Tatar could no more slaughter an unresisting prince than kill a puddle. It wasn't done.

Hence, while the foot soldiers feasted in the streets that night, the Council of the Mongols met to have a few jars of their own and consider what to do.

Batu was a dry old stick and already impatient with the revelry. He wanted to establish order as quickly as possible. If it had been up to him, he would have just thrown Prince Mykhailo in the dungeon and left him there. (The Prince was an irrelevance, militarily speaking. It was Commander Dmytro who had defended Kiev throughout the siege and his head was on a spike at the castle gates while the rest of him was being gratefully devoured by the city's starving canine population.) Batu Khan had no desire to kill Prince Mykhailo, particularly, but he was grandson to the great Genghis, Khan of Khans. He had his reputation to consider.

Later, Weg claimed to have invented the solution but as well as being brutish he was as thick and lumpen as a dung heap. It was his lieutenant Polov who pointed out that the bench at which they were seated was extremely unstable. This was because the Mongols had man-handled it, along with the table, from the state dining room into the Great Hall, so they could eat on the raised dais and witness the cavorting of the lesser officers in the main part of the Hall. One of the bench's broad legs had been knocked out as they had heaved it clumsily through a stone portal. The leg had been pushed back into place but now wobbled dangerously. What was needed was something unresisting to rest upon the leg, before the bench was placed back on it and jammed into place.

Thus the cowardly Prince Mykhailo met his bone-cracking end, as a Mongol's cushion, whereas if he had turned and showed a moment of courage, he could have died swiftly and painlessly in the lap of his beloved Elka.

Thus the long reign of Kiev over the wide steppes of Rus met its nemesis at the hands of the nomads – but in every end, there is a beginning.

Not far from the castle, in a large house belonging to a spice merchant in the trading quarter of Podil, lay a woman called Mina, thirty years old but still beautiful, and in pain.

The cause of her pain need not be mentioned. He is not worthy of a name.

Mina had never married or borne children of her own, content with her role as companion and maid to the merchant and his virgin sister, both of whom lay slaughtered downstairs in the dining room of their splendid home. Mina, like the other servants of the house, had been ravaged, then left to live with it, as the Tatars ransacked the merchant's cellars. Even the

Tatars could tell straightaway that this was the abode of a wealthy man.

Mina lay very still. The room was dark. It had been freezing for months but so many of the streets were burning now that the merchant's house was as warm as a bread oven. Mina lay flat, not daring to move from the position in which the Tatar had left her, feeling the way her skin prickled with the heat and shock of the assault. The pain was unlocated. There was a wide smile of it somewhere between her legs and another small lump of it lodged near her heart. The Tatar had removed his sword but a dagger he wore on a leather strap across his chest had had a lumpy hilt, jewelled perhaps, which had dug into her as he pressed down. It hurt to breathe, so she concentrated on breathing. The pain spoke to her. It said, you are alive.

I am still alive. Many around me are dead and a city is in flames – but I am still alive.

Something else would be alive, soon, inside her, in the unlocatable place beneath the smile of pain.

She would call him Constantine, which was the name her old grandmother Elka once told Mina she had planned to use were she ever unfortunate enough to give birth to a boy.

Trophy Widows

Elena Lappin

'So how long does it take to—'
　　'To get over it?'
I nodded.
'That depends on how good the marriage was.'
She smiled, I smiled, but the truth was, there was
nothing much to smile about. This was a widows' club.
Not one of those support groups led by an opinionated
counsellor of some sort. Just a few women friends (three,
to be exact) who had lost their husbands and were now
alone. Every month or so, they had dinner together,
usually at Barbara's house, and talked about all sorts of
things – anything but *that*. I – a novice – had spent
the whole evening listening to their views on Nigella
Lawson's recipe for chicken soup ('good, but flawed'
was the general consensus), on Jeffrey Archer's peculiar
sex appeal, on his wife's mysterious loyalty and good
legs, and on a racy film called *Confidence* which they
had all enjoyed. 'I couldn't go back to watching all that
silly telly porn after that,' Barbara had declared, sinking
her dainty, bejewelled fingers into a bowl of juicy strawberries. 'This was the real thing. God, how I miss it.'
They'd all laughed and I had joined in, of course, but I
was puzzled. Barbara's husband died ten years ago, she
was now in her mid-fifties, an attractive, deliciously

—[137]—

perfumed, petite brunette with a seductive figure and a big laugh: didn't she have a lover, or ten?

Anne and Karen had gone out into Barbara's small garden for an after-dinner cigarette. She and I were alone in the kitchen, preparing the coffee, and I simply *had* to know: how many days, months, years would it take before I could – before I would want to – start living again? I was quite sure she had the answer.

'What do you mean?' I asked.

'Well, if the marriage was good, it takes longer to get over it, of course,' she said, without taking her eyes off the almost-boiling kettle. 'Sometimes never.'

We were both silent, until the kettle startled us with a loud click of its automatic switch and an escaping cloud of hot white steam.

'How long did it take *you*?' I asked, and immediately wished I hadn't.

'A year. Would you mind carrying the coffee cups? I'll bring the rest.'

I lifted the heavy silver tray she had prepared in advance. It was a gorgeous display of blue and white china, delicate antique silver spoons and forks, a crystal platter holding up the tiara of an elegant chocolate cake with sparkling white icing.

I heard Karen's giggly voice from the living room. 'I never really liked making meals for him, anyway,' she was saying. 'All those red steaks . . . Sometimes it felt like cooking – and drinking – blood! Now I have soups and sandwiches, all day long. And ice cream!'

'And chocolate cake,' she added with zest, when she saw the tray I was carrying. 'Oh my God. Barbara, you angel. You baked this yourself, didn't you? Just being your usual superhuman self.'

'Of course she did,' said Anne, and whispered

conspiratorially: 'She doesn't have much else to do, you know. Not like *us*.'

I knew she meant herself and Karen: they were co-owners of a small shop in Muswell Hill, selling artsy, in-your-face jewellery, some of it made by me, in fact. I supplied them with necklaces and bracelets made of tiny red crystal beads. That was how we met – two middle-aged widows and me, a much younger one. They were both in their late forties, two old school friends, married and widowed at around the same time. Their children were grown up and independent, and Karen and Anne had, somehow, filled the vacuum left by their dead husbands by intensifying their presence in one another's lives. A marriage, of sorts. They had met Barbara and her husband on a Greek holiday, many years ago, and remained friends ever since.

'I heard that,' said Barbara, with a forgiving smile in her voice. 'Coffee?'

I had finally managed to lower the tray onto the glass coffee table, and she bent over the cups, filling them with delicious hot liquid. When I received mine, together with a plateful of chocolate cake and even a scoop of ice cream, I said, 'Thank you,' and burst out crying.

I could feel their silent looks, but no one said anything. I heard slurping, munching, the tinkling of silver spoons against thin china. And, for a long while, not a single word.

Then Barbara said: 'Is it because of what I told you? I'm sorry. But it's the truth. I was very unhappy, before . . . It was . . . a relief, when he died. Still, here I am, all alone, after all these years. Trying to pay a price for not feeling sorry to see him go, I guess. But what I feel really guilty about is that I never told him how unhappy I was, living with him. He should have known the truth. He shouldn't have died believing we had a good marriage.'

'How can you be sure he didn't know you were faking it? Maybe he knew, and didn't want to complicate things. He was such a quiet man, your husband,' said Anne gently, without looking at Barbara. She was staring into her coffee cup, which was still full.

Barbara gave her a sudden, razor-sharp look. Then she smiled, a warmer, less collected sort of smile. I felt a shift in her, as if a weight had lifted. For a moment, it seemed as if a new one had replaced it, but she let it go, and turned to me: 'Did *your* husband know the truth? Tell us.'

I had just filled my mouth with vanilla ice cream, and, as it melted, I began to talk, swallowing ice cream and tears in between my words: 'I don't think so. He guessed it, maybe, but I don't think so. I mean, he *couldn't* know it, because I did everything right, you know what I mean? I was there for him, laughed with him, argued with him, talked about everything . . . The sex, well, it was something he enjoyed and I endured, but I swear, he had no idea. I *liked* him. He was such a good, decent man. But I *loved* the jerk who sent me those hot, dirty emails and made my cunt throb.' I noticed Anne and Karen exchanging satisfied glances, and even Barbara seemed amused.

'I met him only once, at an art fair. He's a photographer and an artist, we had some laughs over a cup of horrible tea in a styrofoam cup . . . And then the emails started, and he went straight for my heart and soul, and I gave it to him, just like that. Heart and soul and cunt, without ever doing it for real. But I was obsessed. Imagine, I would be with my husband, then quickly run to my laptop and say "i love you i love you i love you" to my phantom lover. Except he is not a phantom, he's for real – somewhere. And now my husband is gone, and I'm sure it's my fault he had a heart attack. And I'll never see my email love again, I'll be alone for the rest of my life, paying for what I've done, just like Barbara . . .'

'Hey!' Barbara's even voice stopped me short. 'Leave me out of this. I have my story, you've got yours. Would you like some advice?'

I shook my head. No, I didn't want advice. Not anymore. All I wanted was more chocolate cake, and ice cream, and chocolate cake . . .

'I believe,' said Karen quietly, 'that the greatest gift a married woman can give herself is to have a lover. If there's anything *I* regret about my marriage, it's that I never had one. I knew my husband had the occasional fling, but he loved me or needed me . . . Or maybe both. Who cares . . . But if I had opened up to another man, at least once, I know I would have felt better about myself. There were possibilities . . . Being with my husband was a pleasure, but it was like looking at myself in the mirror – always the same. I really craved to see something new, and I'm sorry I never did. And now he's gone, I regret having been such a coward, such a goddam dutiful, moral, lily-white coward.' She picked up her coffee cup and finished off its contents with one long, determined gulp.

'Let's sum up, then,' said Barbara. 'Seems to me we were all trophy wives, won't you agree? We were all happy to look and act the part of the happy, contented, proper wife, in bed and out of bed. Meanwhile, we all craved something else entirely. And some of us,' she added, glancing in Anne's direction, 'may even have had it. But still – we didn't really mind being trapped, or if we did mind, we never told a soul. Remember the funeral?'

She said 'funeral' as if all of their – all of our! – husbands had been buried together.

'Remember being comforted by family and friends, and even strangers? Remember the fresh, open wound, the loss, the sadness, and how we mourned them all? That was all genuine, of course, regardless. But I wonder, I just wonder . . . A trophy wife never stops playing the part. When her husband dies, she doesn't become a free woman, free to live as she likes. She becomes a trophy widow. Same thing, except with less red meat and more chocolate cake.'

I thought they would all laugh again, but they didn't. They were all silent together, smiling at one another without words. Soon after, we all went home, as if all we'd had was a nice dinner with friends. As if nothing had happened.

But when I came home, I turned on my laptop and searched for an old, unsent message of mine. I had written it the day my husband died. Six months ago. Here it was:

I woke up this morning and you didn't exist. Not for me, anyway. I should have felt relief – isn't that what I've been praying for, ever since you floated into my life like my own private ghost, invisible to everyone else but maddeningly, deliciously real to me? Then, just as suddenly, the ghost was gone and you became a fire that grew and spread and couldn't be contained, unless I let it burn my insides to a cinder. It hurt so much, that fire. It hurt like the most exquisite, sweet surrender. But today, I woke up and felt no pain. This was so unfamiliar I hardly remembered who I was for a moment. Not even my husband's warm curved back touching mine reminded me. Early this morning, your love was neither a distant blur, nor a dagger through my heart; it was – nothing. It wasn't there, because you weren't there. I'd forgotten all about you. So simple. Yet instead of feeling elated at having my old, sane self back, I felt only empty. A blank. And then it passed. It really was just a moment. My husband stirred, I moved a little closer to him, and, as I inhaled his warmth, I remembered – imagined! – yours. That's how I knew I still loved you, and always would. God, all this drama, all this secret turmoil – and all because I was worried there would be no email from you this morning. But there was. There were six messages, your usual average. Ray, my love, you're as solid as a rock. Did I say ghost? Who am I kidding. You couldn't be more real if it were *your* body cradling mine every single night. We moved so fast, didn't we, from cyberbuddies to virtual lovers to . . .what? You're the truest love of my life, and you say I am yours. Bliss, bliss, bliss. Good morning, Ray . . .

I thought of Barbara's chocolate cake, and pressed SEND.

'East Mountain's All Borrowed Light'

❦

Ling E. Teo

'Six a.m. at the station,' she said.

'Six a.m. at the station,' he affirmed.

She hung up the receiver.

For a moment, she felt warmth seeping through her body. Thinking of Li Po, the ancient Chinese poet sleeping in empty mountain, heaven his blanket, earth his pillow.

Empty mountain.

Hers would be Paektu-san, Korea's Holy Mountain, highest in the Taebak on the dividing line between Korea and China. She'd never dreamt that she'd be going there.

She looked forward to being there.

Empty mountain, yet full of the echoes of ravens.

She switched on her laptop and the room glowed with blue light. Another ghost-lit room in the busy Seoul night. She'd lived in this city all her life, assembling guitars at the Gibson International factory. Punctual and meticulous, she was perfect for her job. She liked fitting the parts together into a perfect instrument. They said that the guitar was a dormant object until the hands of an able guitarist brought it to life. Yet the hollow, the bridge and the pegs had especial significance for her.

'Pak Hong-lyong, b. 7.7.1976, Paektu-san', she typed carefully onto a list on the web page. She logged off. The screen flickered, sighed, slept.

She tucked herself into bed, sighed, slept.

She woke up at four in the morning, made a cup of tea and ate the last bean cake. She started to prepare her favourite lunchbox: cold noodles, spring onion salad and barbecued chicken. Lunch and water in bag, hair in place, she put on Bach and sat down to read Li Po. *'Come for the view, I feed on kind winds, new blossoms teaching mind this vast.'*

The verse rose and fell with the fugue and she lost herself in the voluptuousness of the textures, counterpoints and meanings that surrounded her.

The alarm clock rang at half-past five. She prepared to make her way to the station.

Mr Kim was already waiting on the platform, white rose in second button-hole as agreed. He looked carefully groomed for this trip. Nearing fifty years in age, he carried with him a walking stick and an air reminiscent of an orphaned child. The phone call the night before was the first contact they had ever made. She was pleased that they were strangers; this was not a day for familiarity.

'Thank you for coming,' she greeted him sincerely. He nodded his head and answered likewise. Together they boarded the train that was to take them out of the gritty city into the mountains of North Korea. First to the coastal Wonsan, then along the Sea of Japan to Hungnam, Tanch'on, and then inland to Kosongni, Irhyangdong, Hachon and finally to Yapyongdong, where they would alight to make the difficult trek to

Paektu-san. They sat on the right side of the train where the view would be more scenic. She was full of anticipation, couldn't wait to see the sea.

The train soon entered the depths of suburbia ... satellite town, nothingness, satellite town, nothingness. The steady rumble of the engine created a dimension in which her mind roamed freely. She loved trains. She'd always felt that a moving carriage was the best vehicle for understanding existence; there nature, life, sickness and death lost their hard sting. Weightless, she was gliding through a dream. She briefly brushed the measures of space and time, like a cat.

She remembered a time when she was six, maybe seven. Without fail she'd worn white on Mondays, Wednesdays and Fridays; on Tuesdays, Thursdays and Saturdays, blue. And Sundays for her were either pink, the colour of cherry blossoms, or yellow, of big full chrysanthemums. She didn't know why her mind told her to do these tasks, but she did them to the best of her ability because they made her feel protected from mysterious forces. Forces best left unfathomed. In later years, she came to compare that security to the sensation of basking in the glow of reaffirmed affections in a letter, beautifully scripted by a distant lover.

She smiled as she remembered the day she had been *furious* with herself. She must have been about nine years old. That day she'd stepped out of bed left foot first – that week, she'd made a pact with herself to always set out on the *right foot* first thing in the morning – so she'd grudgingly worn a black sweater as penance.

Sometime in her mid-teens, she deliberately departed from the dictations of her head. As she got older she realised that the world wasn't simply sky-blue, cloud-white, chrysanthemums and cherry blossoms. There were crazy human colours too – screaming greens and electric purples, flashy oranges and shocking pinks. They were the colours of the city; colours that *would not be denied*. She gave in to their luminous demands.

In the beginning she'd felt guilty and traitorous for ignoring the rules, but slowly she grew bolder. She remembered the lightheadedness that overwhelmed her when she took her first dance steps in crimson socks. Perhaps there wasn't enough time to simply obey *for there were the thunderstorms and typhoons too*. The cherry blossoms and chrysanthemums, ravaged and destitute, could only fade away in the slag heap of human waste.

Around midday they reached the border between the two Koreas. As expected, customs was very strict. Fortunately Mr Kim, a buckwheat flour merchant who regularly travelled up north for business dealings, was an old hand at the paperwork. She posed as his secretary.

One by one the passengers trailed back onto the train, like sheep barked into obedience. The communist security guards on the platform kept watchful canine eyes, ready to pounce on any irregularity.

The train took a gently undulating course. Humming to herself, Hong-lyong cleaned the window by her seat until it was devoid of even a speck of dust. Slowly and surely the train was beginning its ascent, its surroundings increasingly remote, wild and beautiful. At times the sea peeked through the hills on the right, at times a river flowed rapidly underneath. In these bucolic surroundings the passengers began to unwind, giving in to a power greater than themselves.

'Paektu-san is 2774 meters above sea level,' Mr Kim

addressed her. 'Even if the sea rose two thousand metres, it'd still stand.'

'Global warming,' she concurred. 'Although seventy per cent of Korean land is mountain, most of South Korea would be submerged.'

Mr Kim nodded his head.

They seemed to be able to skip the sentences in between. This made talking effortless, even pleasurable.

'And in the North, island-peaks on a lonely range,' Mr Kim continued. '*Conversations among mountains*.'

'Li Po!' she exclaimed, but wasn't too surprised.

As luck would have it, they chorused the next line of poem in unison, '*There are worlds beyond this one*.'

They both laughed. Slight embarrassment ensued but the ice had been broken.

Mr Kim said, 'Forgive my directness, but you don't seem like an unhappy person.'

'That's because I usually know what I want,' she repaid his frankness.

'Is death what you want, in this moment?'

'To tell you the truth, here, now, I'm just appreciating everything around me.' Instinctively she reached for the single grain of rice left on his lunch plate and washed it down with green tea.

After a while a pensive Mr Kim replied, 'Yes. Nothing is wasted in Nature. All is harmonious. It makes so much sense here.'

They fell quiet, listening to the world around them. Now and again the sound of tumbling waters joined the creaky rhythm of the wheels. The crazy city sounds she had no escape from – engines revving, doors slamming, heels clicking sharply on concrete – became a distant dream. Ever parallel, the railway tracks brought them closer and closer to their destination. Closer and closer, never an inch out of place.

'*A traveller's heart is rinsed in flowing water*': these words stared up at her from her book.

Mr Kim and Hong-lyong were on this journey with the sole purpose of committing suicide together. They'd both wanted to jump into Heaven Lake of Paektu-san, heaven for blanket, earth for pillow. It had been possible for them to arrange this pact through one of thirty 'suicide' web pages back in Seoul. Among some of these pages, poison and cyanide were offered too.

She felt lucky to have found Mr Kim. Since the police began to investigate the 'contract suicides' in which killers could be hired through cyberspace, many websites had been swiftly shut down. Moreover, the adverts for 'suicide partners' had more than fifty thousand hits; to be able to find Mr Kim after only a week had been very fortunate. But above all, *he'd wanted to disappear the same way*.

It didn't bother her that suicide was a thriving business. Most people's lives were completely dominated by deals, so why not death? Death was big business: monks to be hired, monies to be handed out, resting places to be bought. For her, the way mortality and life fed into each other was normal. Sometimes ironic, too. She recalled a parasitic plant choking its supporting source of sunlight and food, only to starve to death later that year.

Many suicides in Korea were failed businessmen. Mr Kim, though, didn't appear too susceptible to market fickleness. The former often revealed themselves by their furrowed foreheads, empty faces and hurried uncoordinated shuffles. Mr Kim was graceful in his gait – he'd practically glided back to his seat from the lunch stall. The fact that he knew poetry also differentiated him from bawdy-humoured, cigar-puffing, middle-aged success. For this reason, she found herself trusting him. Her resolve to remain a stranger on this trip had been shaken by his natural manner and his refreshing straightforwardness.

'Can you tell me why you're here?' he asked.

'It's to do with my grandmother.' Hong-lyong figured they'd come this far together. 'Five years ago, she committed suicide, expressing deep regret that she never saw the Holy Mountain. I'd like to fulfil her last wish.'

'Have you ever thought that she wouldn't appreciate your killing yourself?' he reasoned.

'Yes, but my mind's made up. When I saw what she'd done, I couldn't think of anything else.'

He asked a little tentatively, 'Why did she do it?'

'At the time I didn't understand. But lately I've come across some unsent letters written shortly before her death. She'd been traumatised by the Japanese Occupation when she was taken as a comfort woman. I never knew she had been a comfort woman. Towards the end she couldn't let go. Her body was wasting away, her spirit consumed by the cancer of her memories.'

'I'm very sorry,' he said softly.

They fell silent. Mr Kim lowered his head, as if he were saying a prayer for the many lonely and destitute ex-comfort women of Korea.

Hong-lyong's grandmother had led an exceptional life. Though once brutalised by invading soldiers, she'd enough of her sanity to set up a stable family life. She'd also been brave enough to overcome social barriers to marry her childhood love, partly shaking off the stigma that plagued many comfort women. She never forgot to thank her lucky stars that she had maintained her ability to bear children.

Hong-lyong stared at her crooked thumb which she alone inherited from her grandmother. For as long as she could remember, relatives had always insisted on how she was the image of her grandmother. Hong-lyong felt a strange closeness to her, particularly after her death. As well as the letters, she'd also uncovered scrolls of finger-painting. These intricate paintings invariably depicted flying birds. They were so life-like, so joyous, she wished her grandmother had shown her these paintings when she'd been alive. She remembered that when her grandmother temporarily forgot her pain, she had always shown her kindness and laughter.

The memory brought her back to her purpose on this mission. For a long time, Hong-lyong had believed that she'd outgrown the little girl who carefully tidied her white pinafore on Mondays. She knew that a garment could not guard against the unforeseeable and incommensurable. People could be taken away just as soon as they were bestowed. Everything was relative, *this* she knew. It was Nature's Way. Her intellect informed her that the rat race of Seoul was *no more than* a gradual form of suicide. Most people *chose* to ignore the fact until it was too late. To her mind, Grandma had merely accelerated the end stage of human suffering. Yet how different was her journey from the little white dress? Was this a part of Nature's Way too?

The train moved away from the East Sea and inland towards the rugged brown ridges of the Taebaek. The afternoon sun was turning the slopes orange-yellow, high humidity bestowing the landscape a rich tumescence. Sometimes a stream or pool of water glittered sharply out of the land, striking the path of their vision unexpectedly. The glare was uncomfortable, but she welcomed the invasion.

Mr Kim was asleep on the train, his body slumped over in a relaxed pose. His eyelids twitched from time to time. His lips murmured a semblance of sentences.

Mr Kim was dreaming. Dreaming that he was on a pearl-white beach in Thailand laughing, comfortable with a group of friends. Like the locals, he had a garland of hibiscus around his neck, a sarong around his waist. Then a ladyman – a *koi toi* – walked up to him and asked him what they were having for dinner. Mr Kim woke up abruptly.

Mr Kim was surprised by his dream. All his life he'd lived alone, never interested in relationships. His closest relationship had been with his mother. Through the years, he'd come to believe that he was asexual and commuted his energies to his work. In the larger scheme of things, manufacturing noodles for North Korea from South Korean flour gluts was a meaningful activity, so he'd contentedly done it for many years. He thought of his job as alchemy, changing waste and excess into a valuable and essential commodity. But in recent months, he'd had increasing problems trading with North Korea. More than ever, its corrupt government officials were trying to keep foreign aid to themselves. Exacerbated by the severe droughts in recent years, the number of hungry people in the North had dramatically increased. Faced with these startling problems beyond his control, he felt useless and redundant. With more time than he ever imagined on his hands, he read the books he'd been wanting to read through the years, and began reflecting on his life.

Personally Mr Kim had always felt that something

was lacking in his being. He was a caring person by nature and did his best to help those around him. Yet there was always something tugging at his conscience. He couldn't put his finger on what it was. Since he'd had more time and energy to himself, he'd lost sleep and all sense of balance. It was as if his soul had been cleaved in two a long time ago, and his mind only chose to tell him now. Then one cold winter day the thought of suicide entered his heart, and never left. That murky December afternoon was the only real baggage he brought onto this train.

Mr Kim said to Hong-lyong, 'There are two rivers on the Northern frontier, the Amnok and the Tuman. I guess they'll never meet.'

'One day they will, when the sea rises by two thousand metres,' she pointed out.

He chuckled at the syllogism. Why not, he thought. Who was to say what could happen? He realised this young lady was mature beyond her years, even if she possessed the face of sleeping babies.

Images began to form in her mind's eye. Though fuzzy, Hong-lyong could tell that the images were mainly white. Suddenly they were interrupted by a deep blue pool of water. She recognized it as a picture of Heaven Lake which she had seen in a tourism magazine. Only here, in her mind's eye, the blue was so azure that her senses were forced to tune into its vividness. She wanted the lake to devour her.

Just as suddenly as it had appeared, the image imploded from sheer intensity. Shards of white light emitted rainbow spectrums. In an instant all was black again. She could hear her own short gasps in the darkness. Gradually her senses became clearer, sharper. The same fuzzy white images came into view again.

Instinct told her they were important, but she could not make out what they were.

The light had been changing subtly, transforming the minutiae of the landscape. When Mr Kim caught his breath, he whispered, 'Look, that mountain's the only one left in the light.' Eagerly sharing his secret he revealed, 'It's the favoured peak.'

Instantly, Li Po's verse sprang to her mind. '*East Mountain's all borrowed light*'. She'd read it countless times, only to appreciate its meaning then. Perhaps there the ancient poet once danced, wine gourd by weathered feet, lovingly toasting the moon. She knew that Chang bai shan, where the poet once roamed, was not far to the south-west. Hong-lyong often thought human speech unnecessary; but there on the peak, she took heart from it. The poet's characters, the sounds that accompanied them, conveyed the aura of these mountains so aptly. And yet everything was so sublime, so *unknowable*.

Mr Kim closed his eyes, laid himself back in the Dead Man's pose of Yoga. Limbs stretched out, lips slightly parted, he was trying to drink in the beauty of his surroundings. This seemed to him humanly impossible. As an experiment he'd shut his eyes so as to listen better, but even there his brain could not be stilled. There were too few senses, too little time to experience it all. He wondered if it were possible for Man to fully appreciate his being, to attain harmony on this earth?

'Miss Pak,' he said. 'I comprehend nothing, but I'm glad we came.'

The fuzzy white images came into Hong-lyong's view again. Only this time, they joined up into a recognisable whole. It was her mental picture of a Full Moon Jar, an object she had spent hours observing in a museum. She'd memorised the white porcelain, its slightly asymmetrical form, its bulge showing the seam between the upper and lower halves. She'd scrutinised the cracks which represented its once shattered state, cleverly concealed by an archaeologist's loving hands.

She'd always thought of the Full Moon Jar as epitomising human existence. The artefact was broken, yet it transcended its earthly imperfections. To Hong-lyong, Man's entire being was double-edged. Human talents and skills were nothing short of remarkable, yet the mind was bent on destruction. Most of the time, an individual only very lightly tapped into his or her potential, fleetingly touching the scale of the cosmos. Frequently people forgot that there were powers beyond their experience, dimensions beyond their comprehension.

And there she was on Holy Mountain, Korea's shrine to Nature. Two feet tall and three feet wide, the jar had reappeared, filling up the entire scope of her vision. It was as if a slightly imperfect full moon had descended upon her, just to tell her, Pak Hong-lyong, something important.

Pat-A-Cake, Pat-A-Cake

Tania Casselle

I had the best sex ever when I was fat. Raised by my grandparents after my mother ran off with the Littlewoods pools man and my father committed suicide to punish her, I was built like a sugar baker by the time I was eight. Every morning my grandmother would strap her flowered apron around her waist and roll up her sleeves as if she was going into combat. She cradled the brown china mixing bowl in the crook of her left arm, resting it on her hip like a baby, and tossed in ingredients for fairy cakes with her other hand: flour, soft yellow butter, sultanas, cascades of snowy white sugar, eggs broken with a flick of her wrist against the rim of the bowl. Then she beat vigorously while the flabby undersides of her arm shook in time with the swoopings of the wooden spoon. The cigarette that stuck permanently out of the side of her mouth would grow a long grey ash, trembling over the pale, creamy mixture. I watched, fascinated, waiting for it to drop into the bowl. It never did. At the last possible minute she would pull out the patch pocket on the hip of her apron, take careful aim with the cigarette still glued to her lips, and nod her head sharply. A snake of ash an inch long fell plumb into the pocket and the end of the cigarette glowed red again.

Sometimes she sprinkled the kitchen table with flour and let me cut out gingerbread men with a tin cutter, or she would roll out pastry to fill with apples from the garden. Solid northern cooking, and there was always a treat in my packed lunch or when I ran home from school – a flapjack to keep me going until dinner. Dinner of lamb with fresh mint sauce, roast potatoes, mushy peas and Yorkshire pudding, followed by custardy rice spiked with nutmeg and cinnamon, drowned in pools of single dairy cream.

By the time I was old enough to have boyfriends, I had a roll of pink flesh around my waist, curving thighs as buttery as my grandmother's cooking, but also the advantage of large, plum-shaped breasts that filled out my sweaters and attracted plenty of attention. The boys were relaxed with me. I was less of a threat than my pretty friend Diane who had an aloof attitude to match her lean coltish body. It was easy to progress from friendly walks by the river with Neil or Steven, watching the herons dip to catch fish, to an illicit kiss behind the hedge, a hand surreptitiously wriggling beneath my bra, searching out my plump nipples that hardened in response to hungry hot breath in my ear.

My grandfather promised I'd grow out of my puppy fat, but I didn't. For the whole of my twenties I was always the fattest woman at a party, my underwear the largest to hang, drip-drying over the bath, in my succession of flatshares. I was the girl on the train that people hoped wouldn't sit next to them because my hips overflowed my seat to nudge against their own taut limbs, my thighs puddling out towards theirs. But I refused to wear the clothes the magazines told me I should. I shunned sensible dark colours and vertical stripes and loose-fitting dresses in favour of purple jeans, cherry red velvet tops and butterscotch suede skirts, soft as hot fudge, that caressed my bare legs as I walked. The only black I wore was lace.

It was hard to find the clothes I wanted for the body I had. Some I bought, at a price, through specialist mail order companies. Many I made myself, on the manual Singer sewing machine that my mother had left behind. My grandparents kept it for me and presented it on my fourteenth birthday. I remember looking at its black and gold paintwork and reaching out for the handle that hadn't been touched since my mother's hand last turned it, perhaps while she dreamed of the adventures she might one day have with her pools man. He had been dropping off coupons and picking up the next week's entry for at least a year before the day when he came by and collected her for good.

I made that sewing machine my own, driving it late into the night over satins and crêpes, white broderie anglaise and strawberry velour. Slippery silk jersey slid between my fingers and waterfalled into my lap as I sewed bias-cut skirts, tight as snakeskin, that would hug my round hips and undulate out to a mermaid's tail, skimming the straps of my patent stilettos.

And all that time the sex was great. Men who ogled size 10 women in public went into private raptures over the weight of my breasts, the full moon curve of my behind, the golden delicious ripeness of my shoulders. I loved it. I loved the way a man's eyes glazed over and his mouth opened as I leaned towards him in a bar, the deep cleft above my scooped neckline offering a promise he was not yet sure I would keep. Taking him home and hearing his gasps as he unpeeled me like a fruit, stripping layers of satin and lace, digging into my flesh with greedy fingers, sucking the juice from my core. I would ripple and subside, shiver and roll, for as long as he could bear before the sweetness proved too much and he fell, sticky and gorged, across the dome of my belly. His head salty with sweat next to mine in the cool blue light of dawn.

I worked all this time at a glossy magazine publishing house, sub-editing copy from journalists who ran into the office for an hour at a time to drop off their features before skimming out again to a press reception, a product launch, a cocktail bar opening, a meeting with a contact who had a tip-off in exchange for lunch and good wine at a suitably fashionable restaurant. After all, these were the Thatcher years when the fat cats got fatter and the wide boys got wider and became the *nouveau riche*. Appearance was all, and who you were was not as important as how you looked, what you spent and where you spent it. The magazines kept the world up to date with what was desirable this month, and to do that the writers needed to be out there, spending money, kissing air, flying to Paris, New York, Milan to flirt with the people who counted.

Meanwhile, I was reliable Robyn. The fat girl in the office who wore crazy colours, made funny jokes, brewed good coffee, knew where all the stationery was kept and never lost their copy. I sat alone in the afternoons, head bent over the word processor, typing in hand-scrawled features, correcting spelling and tidying up grammar, punching in witty headlines. The writers, the elite of the magazine hierarchy, knew they could trust me to make them look good, but they never saw me as a threat. How could I be, nibbling my foil-wrapped cheese and ham sandwiches, huddled over my desk like a great fleshy octopus, hands coiling and uncoiling across the keyboard while answering phones and digging out files?

I never mixed socially with the writers. I knew my place. I spent many evenings instead with the advertising salesmen, the layout guys and the production staff. They knew how to drink, starting at 5.30 in the pub over the road and carrying on till closing time, till they could barely stand without spilling their pints, still talking shop and bitching about the publisher and the affair he was having with the fashion editor. Often I would drift away thirty minutes before last orders, go into the next bar down the road and find some company for the night. I knew the minute I walked in whether there was someone I wanted. If not, I left and caught the bus home. But a certain height, a certain gleam of gelled-back hair, a certain glint of white teeth might catch my attention and I would target in, brushing against him with my full swell hips on the way to the bar. It was only a matter of time, sipping slowly, watching him, letting him watch me, before he was separated off from his friends and standing as close as he dared to the crimson heat of my body. On those nights it was a taxi home. Time to get used to a new smell before the final decision of whether to invite him in or to leave him rumpled and unbuttoned in the cab.

The night I met Jack it was raining. The drops bounced from the pavement as we left the pub, splashing my stockings and leaving dark stains on my calves. I showered while he waited for me, then dripped peach-scented lotion between my breasts and dressed again in clean white leather and lilac lace. I generally made it a rule not to see a man more than twice. By then the novelty had worn off on both sides. They were less surprised by the power of my pale skin overflowing raspberry silk, less appreciative. I liked to be appreciated.

With Jack it was different. We met every night for six weeks. He consumed me. His eyes were dark as black grapes and his body thin as a hound. Everything about him was long, and his arms stretched right around my waist and made me feel lost and found all at once. When I had my period he just lay next to me, running his finger along the pink indents on my stomach left by my underwear. He told me stories about pirates and mermaids and treasure until I fell asleep. As soon as we could make love again he took me to the theatre, and in the dark ran his tongue up and down the fingers of my left hand, licking across the wide-stretched webs between them until I was wet. The play was a murder mystery. But I never found out who dunnit.

The last day we spent together we'd planned to go to the coast to swim and fish and make love on the sand like in a film, but we'd stayed in bed much too late to make the trip. Instead we ordered in sushi and ate it in the bath while I sang sea shanties and Jack dived for pearls beneath the suds. The bath was quite a tight fit for both of us, especially when Jack decided to re-enact *Jaws* with my ankle, and we soon transferred back to my big double bed. It was a short day and a long evening, and I fell asleep early, Jack's dark curls still damp against my shoulder.

The bedroom was very hot when I awoke in the middle of the night. The gas heater had been left on and I'd thrown the sheets back in my sleep. Under my half-closed eyelids I could see Jack crouching naked over my hips, watching my breasts rise and fall. He was obviously unaware I'd woken up. His shadow from the glowing lamp, its light soft as honey, was thrown across my face. I lay in his dark shade and looked at him. Even in the drowsy heat, his intense gaze made me apprehensive;

the tension in his clamped tight jaw was unnerving. I shivered and sensed the fine hairs standing up on my exposed thighs. He breathed warm against them, smoothing the hairs down with the flat of his palm so I could hardly feel it, and started to murmur very softly. At first I couldn't hear what he was saying and I didn't want to move my head in case he realised I was listening. Then, as he ran the tip of his finger up the white under-sheet in the triangle of space between my open legs, scrupulously avoiding contact with my skin, I began to pick out his words.

'Pat-a-cake, pat-a-cake, baker man . . .' Jack crooned to himself, rocking gently on his haunches as he traced his fingers over the V of my pubic hair, half an inch away from touching me. 'Bake me a cake as fast as you can . . .' I could see between his legs a hardness growing and he reached down slowly to stroke it, his face masked in a grimace. 'Pat it and prick it and mark it with B . . .' His back suddenly arched upwards like a cat hissing on a fence. He straddled my right thigh, balancing on his knees and one hand while the other hand worked franti-cally. His spidery limbs hunched over me and saliva spun in a single thread to hang glistening from his chanting lips. 'And put it in the oven for Baby and me . . .' the last was breathed out in a whisper as his open mouth lowered, sharp teeth glinting towards my belly.

I jerked away, pulling my legs up towards the pillows, grabbing at the sheets to cover me. Jack looked up. His eyes were fire and his lips too red as he smiled. We didn't say a word. I was trembling and so was he, but differently. For a moment the stillness of the air seemed to seep into my every pore. I was as motionless as a wasp drowned in beer, captured in the hazy golden glow of the room. Then I was free and away, turning off the gas heater, opening the windows to let in the midnight breeze and splashing cold water on my burning face.

When I came back, Jack was still smiling. He lifted his glass of red wine from the bedside table, raised it towards me wordlessly as if in a toast, and drank it back in one long, lazy swallow. I went out of the bedroom, opened the front door and stood by it as I waited. Jack dressed without haste and smoothed his hair in the hall mirror before he left, wiping a small stain of wine from the side of his mouth.

It took nine months to lose the weight my grandfather had told me was puppy fat. It was a hard discipline and left me dizzy with hunger. I dreamed every night of plump scones, thick damson jam and sweet whipped cream, and woke up in the morning to a glass of water and thin dry toast. As I ran the rainy city streets, pushing my legs for another mile, I pictured the fat being washed off me, dripping from the pavement and running into the gutters, where it gathered in white greasy clumps in the drains, feasted on by rats.

As my body tightened into bone and muscle I began to wear only black and white and shades of grey. I shopped for sharp tailored suits in crisp gabardine, severe flannel skirts that outlined the spikes of my hip-bones and jackets as angular as my coat-hanger shoulders. My mother's sewing machine grew dusty on the table until I gave it away to a jumble sale for the old people's home. In its place I put a large cactus plant in a matt black pot.

At work, the magazine writers grew less friendly as I stopped making their coffee and started suggesting my own features: stories better than the ones they flung across my desk each day and which, in the new dawn of cost-cutting and down-sizing, relied less on expensive lunch-fuelled tip-offs. I became the publisher's darling, working long hours and turning in impeccably economical stories written in the spare, pithy style that has since become my trademark. In fact, the publisher soon dumped the fashion editor and started sleeping with me. Now Michael and I are seen together at all the right parties, arriving late and leaving early and never drinking too much, as we both like to be in the office by 7.30 am. But we do have a rule to keep Sundays free of business. It's our time to work out together in our home gym, visit the modern art galleries or browse around antique shops to add to our collection of Netsuke. I expect one day we will marry. The writers for whom I'd once typed copy and booked taxis cannot afford to be overheard attributing my rapid promotion to nepotism, however, as I now employ them.

You could say that as the editor of a leading style magazine that is gratifyingly fat with advertising, I have the world on a plate. And I do. But the sex? Well, I close my eyes and remember the time when my breasts were as round as the sky and my thighs thick as trees, and my flesh surged and swelled like the sea.

The Second Coming of Sara Montiel

Patricia Duncker

Carmen was busy painting her nails on the plane. She sucked her teeth and swore when Easyjet hit a pocket of turbulence and her aim slipped. Pepper patted her knee and made soothing noises. He had his eyes tight shut and his teeth clenched.

'Is all right, gal.'

'I'm not scared of flying anymore, boss. Why? You nervous?'

She looked at him carefully. Something was horribly wrong. Was he going to be sick?

'It's not so bad if you open your eyes.'

Pepper ogled the nail polish. Purple Passion. An evil, suggestive colour which became fluorescent under the spots. He had given her the pot and the lipstick to match. They were flying to Barcelona, scene of his greatest sexual triumph, when he had pulled the most gorgeous Arab boy in the bar. Pepper was barely present beside Carmen in the plane. He was reliving those first ecstatic moments of dawning passion when he had entered La Concha, in search not of sex, but literary vibrations.

'Genet used to drink here,' he gushed to the bored boy dressed as a '40s Hollywood star.

'Who's Genet?' demanded Hassan, concentrating on his nail polish.

'He's a Great Writer. He made our lives possible.' Pepper had read *A Thief's Journal* under the bedclothes with a torch as a teenager and had never recovered from the experience. Hassan raised his superb, curling lashes in an incredulous, languid stare.

'Well, he may have made them possible, but he didn't make them easy.'

How rich was this black tourist, who spoke English but clearly wasn't American? Hassan assessed the cost of the flash jeans with flares, the embroidered belt and the rings bulging with red stones. Not costume jewellery. He had an unlikely hat perched on the back of his Afro, but had taken off the shades when he walked into the bar. Hassan noticed that the man's eyes were dark brown and wet with emotion. This guy was for real. Could he risk asking for champagne?

'You loved this Genet?' he crooned sweetly. Genet was probably one of the black man's ex-lovers.

'He is a genius,' sighed Pepper.

'Did you drink champagne here together?' Hassan assumed a wheedling tone.

'I think he drank rum.'

'Ah. Well, I'd like a Campari cocktail,' Hassan decided.

Pepper looked up and saw a god in full-length blue sequins and Purple Passion nail polish, smiling down upon him.

And so it all began. Hassan was as fickle as he was gorgeous. Pepper's frequent trips to Barcelona often ended in scenes, tears and rage. All the money got spent on dresses never worn above three times or, in the later days, on coke. The odd thing about Hassan was that he went on looking as if he were seventeen when he was certainly pushing thirty. Pepper suspected him of having a picture in the attic. Then one day the begging phone calls ceased. Pepper scrambled onto the next flight to Spain.

Hassan had simply vanished. The flat was empty, all their life together packed up and removed. Pepper could get nothing out of the whores at La Concha. No, they hadn't seen Hassan. No, his mother and sister hadn't been over from Morocco. What with the amount of coke he was snorting it wasn't strange if he vanished for a while, often weeks at a time. No, not at all surprising. There were rumours, of course. Hassan had found another rich protector and become a kept woman. He had encountered a married couple on a yacht and was last seen screwing both of them. He had heard the call of the muezzin and gone to fight the French in the desert. No one really knew where he had gone. He became one of the disappeared.

Pepper never got over this Arab boy. Pepper had fallen in love. He failed to notice the fact that Hassan wanted nothing more than a bottomless pocketful of cash. Pepper had other men, but he never loved anyone else other than the Arab whore with long lashes and pretty dresses. After the loss of Hassan, as a displacement activity, Pepper went on to make a fortune in the music industry. Carmen was his most lucrative discovery. He found her singing Bessie Smith cover versions upstairs at Ronnie Scott's. He listened carefully to her smoky supple voice, then offered her a lift home. He made her a proposition in the taxi, rather different from the one she was expecting. She had to give up smoking, put on four stone, let him pay for a year's worth of singing lessons with a maestro of his choice and sign her soul away to Hot Island Records for ever and ever.

She was as sulky as Hassan, and just as obstinate. She mounted a huge battle about putting on weight. Pepper told her that she looked like a drug-addicted stick and that he couldn't market a blues singer who hadn't any tits. Carmen's mother pitched in on his side. She didn't think that thin women were beautiful. Thinness was a whitewomanting. And she had heard tell of Pepper's father, Reginald Leroy Jones, who came from Trinidad. As did her husband, God rest his soul.

Carmen's mother stood beside Pepper, shaking her head at Carmen's recalcitrance. Carmen gave up smoking and put on four stone almost immediately. She moved downstairs at Ronnie Scott's and caused a sensation. Pepper was a generous man. When the money, contracts and offers of international tours descended on them in a waterfall, he altered her contracts and upped her percentage, still keeping the lion's share for himself. He became her manager. She lost her sleazy, sleepy look and shone like a well-brushed panther on display in a circus. Pepper dressed her up, took care of all the details. He insisted on buying all her performance clothes. She was fantastically and extravagantly clad. Pepper's taste leaned towards exaggeration and excess. Carmen drew the line at strapless orange taffeta. She stripped it off in front of him, proving that the four stone were genuine. Pepper never laid a finger upon her. He was queer to the marrow of his bones and had never laid a finger upon any woman. He could smell the difference.

They stayed in 5-star hotels. Carmen's jewellery had to be locked away in the safe when they arrived. She always wore it on the planes in case she needed to bargain with hijackers. For the only thing Pepper could not bring himself to spend money upon were the planes. He rang up obscure bucket shops or bustled round the internet, scouring the airlines for better deals. When they flew to Montreal for the first time in 1988 he discovered a bargain charter for £99 return. But Carmen found out that they were leaving from Luton at three in the morning and threw the mother of all wobblies. Pepper's meanness prevailed. The hotels became more luxurious and the economy charter bargains stayed the same. They were now cruising down to Barcelona on a ticketless Easyjet holiday flight.

Carmen was singing at a club called American Diva. The show had been sold out for weeks in advance. Pepper extended the tour by three performances. These sold out too. Pepper demanded more money. Carmen's mother rubbed her hands, delighted. American Diva was in a hot pocket of the city called El Born. Pepper saw her through the first night. He left her in the care of her bodyguard for the second. Carmen never had nervous fits. She was a perfect professional down to her Purple Passion fingernails. Her confidence was a little sinister.

Carmen's only weakness was men. If a man gazed longingly upon the now ample, handsome tits and besieged her dressing room with flowers and champagne, she was appallingly likely to say yes. After a dreadful incident with a Norwegian pervert, who had smeared her body with crushed avocados, Pepper hired the bodyguard. He was a completely silent Japanese man named Gus. Gus nurtured a torrid homosexual passion for an Englishman whom he rang up every night. So far as he was concerned Carmen was a tricky assignment rather than a temptation. He drove her cars and sat behind her on the bucket shop charter flights. He monitored her phone calls, policed her autograph sessions, purchased her condoms and checked her premises for lurking suitors. He informed Pepper that his job would be a lot easier if Carmen could be persuaded to have a regular boyfriend rather than an endless saga of one-night stands. Gus was not interested in spontaneous passion.

'Yeah, yeah,' said Pepper. He knew Gus was right. But he still remembered a night in a bar in Barcelona at the beginning of the 1970s when he was wearing flares and an Afro, and an Arab boy in full-length blue sequins, and then later that same night, in daring, strapless orange taffeta, had captured his heart.

Pepper stopped behind a flower stall to score two interesting white tablets off an American crusty.

'This'll set you up, man. Have a great night.'

Pepper went striding back down memory lane. He turned off the Ramblas and passed over to the other side – the darker side of the streets.

Carmen looked for Pepper in the bar. He wasn't there. When she came offstage he was always there. She looked around for Gus. He was sitting impassively in front of an orange juice. A crowd of fans rushed at her, waving their CDs: Carmen Campbell, Best Of. Gus lurched off his seat and thugged them up into orderly lines. The signing and smiling took an hour and a half. The music journalists took up another hour. By the time she was free it was almost two in the morning. Pepper was still not there and Carmen was hungry enough to eat the hotel curtains.

'Where the fuck's the boss gone, Gus?'

'He's looking for his lost love,' said Gus, gloomily. This was the longest speech that Gus had ever made. Carmen looked at him, astonished.

'Lost love?'

'Hassan.'

The name had never passed Pepper's lips in front of Carmen.

'Hassan?'

'La Concha. Genet drank there.'

Gus lapsed back into monosyllables.

'Who's Jenny?' snapped Carmen, looking down at her Purple Passion nail polish, which was ever so slightly chipped. Lost love was bad news. So were spontaneous trips down the dark pathways of the past.

'Order a car, Gus. We're going out to find the boss.'

The bar was still there, exactly where it had been thirty years before. He remembered Hassan's sunburnt skin, warm as the nap of a ripe peach. He opened the door and for a second, saw a room full of men and excessively beautiful transvestites, all dressed like film stars. It was like stepping onto a Hollywood set. There were the shimmering harem bead curtains, the back rooms smelling of spilt sex, the rough boys in leather with their shaved heads and obscene tattoos, and there he stood handsome in the doorway, slick as a Mafia boss in a dinner jacket and spats.

The bar was still there.

But it was almost empty. The curtains were still there, but they were drawn aside and looped up like a bourgeois kitchen separation screen. The sagging couches smelled not of sperm, but of damp. The whole dank cavern was dilapidated and sad. There were eight men clinging to the bar, some Arab, some Catalan, and no one was under fifty. The Nigger of the Narcissus stood behind its shining length. He had huge muscles, earned heaving weights in the gym, a golden smile and a single earring. He had grey hair.

The disco crystal was still circulating in empty space above them. Many surfaces had flaked away; others were blackened and cracked. The photographs of Sara Montiel were still there. Here she was laughing with James Dean, luscious on the arm of Gary Cooper. Pepper put on his glasses. The portraits were yellowing. Some of them were creased and slightly stained with damp. Pepper shrugged himself onto the bar stool and struggled to remember not only who he had once been, but who he now was. He had inadvisedly swallowed both of the white tablets at once. Everyone said Hello. Pepper nodded. He ordered whisky. He then set about losing his mind, entirely and forever.

'Is this your first time in Barcelona?' proposed the handsome black barman, acting as elderly hostess among the senior statesmen ranged along the stools.

'Genet used to drink here! Did you know that?' roared Pepper. The barman flashed his golden smile and indicated a frightful photograph of Genet in a hat perched just behind the bottles.

Pepper stared into his idol's ancient creased face and glassy eyes. The picture was dingy and curled. Above the raddled image of the old writer Pepper saw his own face in the spotted dirty glass. He too was old. He had lost one tooth and was now sporting a pink gap. The boys who clustered round him in the studio wanted to be on the covers of the CDs he produced, not in his bed. His stomach bulged suggestively over his underpants. He could just see the emerging roll beneath his shirt. He had developed an ingrown toenail. He could no longer seduce, he could no longer charm. On the other side of the bar was nothing but a black abyss.

Everyone else strewn along the stools watched Pepper's existential crisis developing with expressions of perceptive sympathy. They had long since crossed the bridge towards which Pepper was advancing with rapid strides and substantial help from dramatic slugs of neat whisky. The white tablets began to take hold. Pepper started to rant uncontrollably.

'I was queer before gay,' he thundered, 'Queer! Does anyone remember queer?'

Everyone listened, puzzled, but interested.

'Is he one of the immigrants on hunger strike?' asked one of the bar's permanent inhabitants in Catalan when it became clear that Pepper was monoglot English. The barman concluded that he must be since he was black and gripped by a great passion. He drew Pepper's attention to their stack of supporting leaflets.

Around midnight the door lurched open and a lovely upbeat drag queen came swinging into the bar. He kissed and greeted all the men in turn and by name, offering his hand to Pepper as well in the convivial embrace. Pepper looked into the man's painted face and saw the lines and chasms beneath the cultivated surface. He too was old, old.

'*Mon semblable, mon frère,*' screeched Pepper and fell off the bar stool.

'*Comment ça va?* How're you doing, man?' said the drag queen cheerfully, trying out several languages and arresting Pepper's descent onto the murky damp of the composting carpet.

'I am Sir Percival Leroy Jones,' shrieked Pepper, giving himself a gong on the spur of the moment.

'No offence meant,' smiled the drag queen, helping him up. He hadn't understood a word, but correctly identified Pepper as an amiable colourful drunk. He rattled a charity can under Pepper's nose.

'For the AIDS ward and the research unit. One of my

friends works there,' he added, giving the request for money a personal touch.

The row of men fumbled in their pockets. Pepper realised that he had misjudged the company. They were reaching for their guns. He dived towards the floor and skidded down into a mass of discarded fag ends. Then the grille upon the door rattled as if it were being shaken by a mighty wind. It was too dark for Carmen to see the door handle and she was trying to force the grille. Someone sitting near the door opened it for her and she stepped down three stairs into the murky space, lifting her gown above her high heels.

So far as the bar was concerned it was the Second Coming of Sara Montiel. Before them stood a transsexual so lovely she could have been a woman, in full-length blue sequins, her golden cloak edged with fur, flung back to reveal a dark ravine between her olive breasts, high, proud and pointed like restored gargoyles. Her hair was piled up in a series of predatory coils. It was a wig, but didn't look as if it was.

'Hassan!' shouted Pepper from the depths.

He was sitting in a puddle of slopped Baileys. Here at last was his Beloved. Someone had told the errant youth that his Master had returned. The boy had dressed to kill, then rushed out to be re-united with his lover, to drink champagne and snort coke in an ecstasy of joy.

'What're you doing down there, boss?'

Carmen hauled Pepper to his feet. She saw at once that her manager had long since passed the point of no return and was almost certainly hallucinating. She looked around. Good God, what an awful place.

The Nigger of the Narcissus beamed at the new arrival. He was relieved that someone else had come to clear up Pepper. The gorgeous transsexual was a blast from the radiant past, when there had been singers every Friday and Saturday night to accompany the sexual struggles behind the harem curtain. She was elegant, expensive, one of the up-town whores.

'Champagne?' he suggested.

Carmen was delighted to have discovered the missing prodigal. The boss was clutching her hand in a way he had never done before. He was alarmingly cross-eyed. But she was in the mood to celebrate.

'Champagne for everyone,' she cried.

'Are you an actress or a singer?' asked one of the punters, speculatively staring at Carmen's crotch. Did he still have his tackle? Or had he gone for the op? Pepper lifted his head off the bar.

'That's my boyfriend,' he growled. Hassan had painted his nails with Purple Passion nail polish, just as Pepper loved them best. Purple and blue sequins in his dress. Purple eye shadow. Purple lips. A little stagy perhaps, but ravishing. He smelt a little odd. Pepper sniffed the air.

'I love you, my darling.' He leaned over and shot her a most terrific ogle.

'You're out of your head, boss,' snapped Carmen, lining up the glasses all along the bar.

'Give us a song, sweetheart,' urged the drunken punter. Carmen slapped down two notes of 10,000 pesetas and waved away the change. The Nigger of the Narcissus turned off the pounding disco music. They all heard the feeble thump of the central heating clicking in. The bar darkened, held its breath, closed like a clam around ten old and drunken men, beached in history, gazing at this huge olive-skinned transsexual with breasts like the statue of Diana at Ephesus. Standing at the bar, Carmen straightened her back, steadied her shoulders. The aged drag queen was admiringly fingering her cloak. Breathe. Sing something they all know.

She looked round the walls and came face to face with a white woman wearing clothes identical to her own. There she was, laughing with James Dean, loving up Gary Cooper. Breathe. Sing. Something they know. Breathe.

> *Do not forsake me, oh my darling,*
> *On this our wedding day*

The crowd sighed with pleasure. Many of them joined in.

> *I'm not afraid of death*
> *But oh, what will I do if you leave me?*

Pepper gazed at Hassan. At last. The boy had understood and shared his pain. Hassan had never forgotten him. He had no idea that Hassan could sing. It was a little odd.

Carmen's voice rushed into all the damp corners where illegal partners had savaged one another's bodies, loveless, uncaring. She filled every man's heart with hope that tonight he would meet the one he loved and somehow they would know that it was to be this time, this place, now.

> *Do not forsake me, oh my darling,*
> *You made that promise when we wed,*
> *Do not forsake me, oh my darling,*
> *'Til I have shot Frank Miller dead.*

Pepper felt a rush of jealousy. Who was this Frank Miller

Hassan was singing about? Had the boy met a white man at the clinic? Was this the chap in the white coat, who organised his hormone treatment? He glared at Carmen. The bar vibrated with applause.

The row of men toasted Carmen with the champagne she had bought for them and yelled for more. Hearing the shouts from the bar in the street outside several young men wandered in and were immediately absorbed into the general atmosphere of conviviality and free booze. It's open house tonight. We are all young and in love. Carmen sang 'La vie en rose', 'I Did it My Way' and 'Je ne regrette rien', with an obligatory bass choral accompaniment. The bar was flush with sentimental passion and the big, big love that fills everyone who has drunk half a dozen glasses of free champagne.

Pepper was exceedingly unsteady on his feet. The white tablets flared through his system in one final burst.

'Last song, boys!'

Carmen raised her glass to the assembled men. She tried out an old Seekers number, which her mother used to sing when she was doing the hoovering.

> *My love, the light is dawning,*
> *This will be our last goodbye,*
> *Though the carnival is over*
> *I will love you till I die.*

Pepper surged away in the direction of total unconsciousness on a wave of ecstasy. Hassan had never declared himself so unconditionally. He collapsed at his lover's feet.

The elderly Moroccan whores carried Pepper, who was still singing 'You'll never walk alone' in a whispered cracked falsetto, outside to Gus and the waiting taxi.

Before he descended into darkness Pepper knew that he was being transported by a seductive handsome man, half his age, the only man he had ever loved. His exit was applauded by everyone standing in the doorway of La Concha. He was in triumph.

Jacob's Tree

Ravai Marindo

The telephone was ringing as I entered the flat. Diving through heaps of books, papers and narrowly missing my lazy cat, Febby, lying on its bean bag, I plucked the phone off the wall and crashed into a chair, swearing and answering in a breathless voice at the same time. My 'Hello?' was followed by silence and the sound of static. Impatiently, I went into a series of hellos and was just about to put the phone down when it dawned on me that the static and silences could be due to a long distance connection rather than a phone pest.

I slowed down and listened. Then I heard a short laugh and the voice of my twin sister coming thinly through the line. 'Well, my dear, I see nothing has changed. You sound as chaotic as usual...What was that racket over there – the chaos that can be heard thousands of kilometres away?'

I laughed and carried the phone to a comfortable chair. It was very rare for my sister to call from Harare. Her theory was that I should call from London as it was cheaper and easier. Cheaper? I don't know how she passed through university with such poor understanding of economics. However, as a lawyer, she had never lost an argument. I would call her ten times in a year, and she would call me once.

'Listen, Tendai' – silence . . . static – 'you have to come home.' – Gap . . . static – 'They have taken our land. I mean, some people have resettled themselves illegally in the farm and I need you here.'

I couldn't believe it. She was doing it again. Somehow or other she looked for reasons to pull me back home. She expected me to travel thousands of kilometres to fight for a piece of land that meant very little to me. Did it matter who settled on the land? After all, both of us have careers that have nothing to do with land. I have no love for old farm buildings with no water or electricity, hills, savanna grasslands and dust. I felt the umbilical pull coming into force, and tensed up, preparing for a fight.

I came back to the thin voice on the line and decided that I had better end it there and then. I was not going back home.

I took a deep breath and speaking slowly, said, 'My final practical examination is in two weeks' time. I cannot travel to Zimbabwe. I have to prepare now.'

'Tendai, they have settled in the valley and have put a shack beneath Jacob's Tree.'

Silence from both sides. Only the sound of breathing. I waited for her to say something. The war of silence. We used to practise that as kids, just staring at each other, eyes bulging, and seeing who lowered their head. She always gave up before me and would give me a hug.

'I'll book my ticket and let you know soonest.'

'I'll pick you up at the airport.'

So it was all arranged. In three days' time I was on a British Airways flight, flying thousands of kilometres towards my rural roots.

*

'When picking mushrooms, you have to use your sense of smell, sight and touch. Poisonous mushrooms smell different from non-poisonous ones. They feel different too, rubbery and sometimes very powdery and they look ugly, sometimes sickly yellow like festered wounds . . .'

My grandmother Gogo's voice droned on and on. We were walking on the red hill overlooking what my sister and I called the valley of the mushrooms. The tops of the forest trees appeared like an impenetrable green carpet in front of us.

As usual, Tanya and I were holding hands. I was making faces at Gogo's back, with Tanya giggling at my antics. Funnily enough, although Tanya appeared not to listen to what Grandma was saying, she always remembered minute details about plants, mushrooms, when to cross the river, herbs for a headache, for bee stings, and for snake bites. From a young age, she had this incredible capacity to absorb and remember details. Yet, I would end up as a doctor and she as a lawyer.

We were thirteen years old, attending school at a cold Catholic establishment where mushroom picking and herbal knowledge were definitely not in the syllabus. Holidays at the farm were always different and exciting. With so many animals, plants, cows, goats, sheep, crocodiles, hippos, it was pretty wild. Then there were Grandma's stories to add spice to life. I did not believe many of her stories, but they made good listening.

'Are we going to Jacob's Tree, then?' I asked Grandma. She kept quiet and continued walking.

'Why is it called "Jacob's Tree", Gogo?' Tanya asked.

Gogo walked to the top of the hill and sat down. We sat on each side of her, watching the sun set over a clear, blue horizon. The sun grew bigger and redder as it moved down until it was a flaming red ball in the sky.

Then all of a sudden it sped downwards, hid behind the hills and a velvet darkness began to fall over us, enveloping us in its soft warm interior, the music of night insects getting louder around us. We sat there, not seeing each other but feeling the warmth emanating from each other's bodies and Grandma's voice blending with the night as she sang and told stories about the cleverness of the hare and the stupidity of the baboon. Then Gogo's mood changed and she became serious.

'Today I am going to tell you a true story about where the tree got its name.' We drew closer to her and she put an arm around each of us.

'A long time ago, a young girl of your age was given into marriage by her parents to a rich elderly man. Nobody told her that she was getting married. She was very happy when her father took her to the store and bought her the first new dress she ever owned.'

Gogo smiled. 'It was the colour of the setting sun, and soft to touch. The girl felt like a princess when she wore it. She rushed to her mother to show her the dress, but found her mother crying her eyes out. A few days later, an aunt and uncle walked with her a long distance to a foreign homestead. They arrived late at night and the young girl was told to go and sleep with the children of this strange household.'

Gogo cleared her voice, then continued with her story. 'When she woke up the following morning, her aunt and uncle were already up and ready to travel back. The young girl rushed indoors to pick up her mat and small bag of clothes. Her aunt followed her indoors and told her not to take her goods because from then onwards she belonged with this new family. The aunt also told her not to degrade her family and to stay, work and listen to everything she was told. The aunt and uncle went away.'

'The girl was not allowed to play with other children, but expected to work with older women. At night, a man whom she thought was a friend and was nice to her during the day, did horrible, painful things to her.'

'For many days afterwards, the young girl tried to run away to go back to her family, but they always managed to catch her and bring her back. Each time they brought her back, the "new mother" would lock her up without food for two days and tell her she would be fed only if she behaved herself and did not try to run away again. The young girl cried for a long time. She tried to tell the "new mother" that she had no problem being a daughter if only that big man, her son, didn't do painful things to her at night. The new mother told her to shut up about things that happen at night or something bad would happen to her.'

'The young girl kept on hoping for a saviour from her family. Once, her uncle came for a visit and she rushed to him and told him all. He told her to shut up about such shameful things and to be a good girl. It was then that the uncle told her that the man was her husband, and she should do what he wanted. In the end, the girl gave up. She ran out of steam, got tired of escaping, and finally faced the reality that her family didn't want her back.'

'Things got better. The man became kind to her and her new mother began to give her less work, especially when she complained of stomach aches.'

Then Gogo kept quiet. It was as if she had physically left us, or as if my sister and I had only conjured her. The night was becoming darker. I could barely make out the shadow of Jacob's Tree that dominated the valley. I could hear all the frogs in a chorus, following the lead singer, some in tenor, others in bass. I heard different birds adding to the night noises, then a wild dog, a leopard and jackals.

'Gogo . . .'

'Sh . . . shh . . .' she replied. 'Let's enjoy the silence. Let's enjoy the night.'

We sat like that for a while. In the silence and darkness, I envisaged the young girl. I heard her sing her loneliness in the valley. I felt a connection with her.

Grandma stood up, stretching her legs and arms, looking like a long dark ghost in the night.

'It's getting dark, let's go back,' she said to us.

She held our hands and we walked slowly back. Tanya and I begged our grandmother to finish her story but she refused, saying, 'There is always tomorrow. I will tell you the next time when we sit on that hill again and watch the sun go down, why that tree is called Jacob's Tree.'

My grandmother died without ever finishing her story. My father died before her, so my sister and I inherited the farm, the red hill and Jacob's Tree.

My flight to Harare was rather uneventful, or rather what was happening externally was inconsequential compared to the turmoil inside me. I thought that when I left Zimbabwe, I could shed my roots like a python shedding its old skin.

My sister was waiting at the airport for me. She hadn't changed one bit, and was as tall and thin as before. The only new thing about her were the glasses, which made her look more of a real lawyer than all the certificates in her office.

We immediately drove to the farm, which was 200 kilometres from the city.

I was sweating profusely, my heart beating very fast, and I felt extremely nervous. I had not been back to the farm for five years, and I felt more nervous the closer we got.

'How are you feeling?' my sister asked me, with a lot of kindness in her voice. 'It must be hard coming back after such a long time.'

I grunted something in reply. It seemed that the closer we got to the farm, the more I lost my power of speech.

'Sit back, Tendai, and take a deep breath. Let nature heal you. Just look at the savanna woodlands as we drive by. Try not to think.'

I wanted to scream at her – 'What do you know? You think it's easy to carry secrets and to come back to a place you considered dead and buried forever?'

My sister kept quiet for a while. Then turning to me, she said, 'Don't shut me out. I am just as hurt as you. You know, one thing I never understood was why you never cried. He was your father too.' Her voice was quivering, full of tears.

I kept quiet. How can words express an emotion? Sometimes it is easier to leave it all inside, to fill one's life with experimental scientific work, which can be controlled in the laboratory. I wish I hadn't come back.

We arrived at the farm late in the night. Everything was pitch black, and I couldn't identify the position of the houses. We were too tired to even think of eating or drinking, we just took a torch, unlocked one of the rooms and crashed on the floor. I could smell the dust on the floor, in the air, everywhere. All through the night, I heard sounds of little animals running across the room. In my imagination, all of have them had razor sharp teeth and shaggy hairs with poisoned ends. I saw a million eyes in the darkness.

We woke up early and walked to the red hill. Tanya knew exactly where the illegal people had settled. We stopped at the red hill and looked down at Jacob's Tree. As we stood there I felt the years roll away.

My stepmother's voice was screaming at me as usual.

'Tendai, come back here. Don't you realise you are a grown-up girl now? You have to contribute to this household. Do your bit. I want you to go and fetch water now!'

I ignored her shrill voice and kept on running, faster and faster towards the hill. Reaching the top, I looked behind to check whether she was following me, but all was clear. Even my two half-brothers, who tried to make all my private business theirs, were nowhere in sight. I sighed in contentment at the prospect of reading a romantic novel in silence, in a sibling-free environment.

I then sat down, pulled out a Mills and Boon book from under my sweater, and settled down to some good, undisturbed reading. After a while, I raised my head and looked directly down the valley towards Jacob's Tree.

At first I thought my eyes were deceiving me, but yes, there was something hanging on the tree. It seemed to be swinging in the wind.

I rushed downhill towards the valley, calling to Tanya as I did so, although I had left her at the homestead. The downhill momentum pushed me faster and faster until I found myself standing under Jacob's Tree, which was at the lowest point in the valley. I raised my head and came face to face with the bulging eyes of my father. He was hanging from the tree, with a thick rope around his neck. His trousers had fallen off and his shirt was hanging askew.

After the initial shock and horror, I only knew that I wanted to dress my father and make him look decent. I climbed up the tree, reached out and struggling, untied the rope around his neck. He fell on the ground as stiff as a piece of wood. Using my fifteen-year-old strength, I pushed the body under some bushes. I then ran home and told Tanya that she had to come with me because someone had killed our father.

It was Tanya, crying and bellowing like a cow, who rushed the whole homestead to the place where I had left him. I had hidden the rope that he used to hang himself. Even in death, I was concerned with his appearance.

Later, my grandparents brought the police to investigate. An accused had to be found. My grandparents were wealthy enough to influence the outcome of the investigation. It was through their contribution that a man called Ezekiel, who used to work as a labourer, was tried and found guilty of murder, receiving fifteen years' imprisonment.

Why did I keep quiet? I don't know really. I suppose I did want someone to be punished. Since it wasn't my father, it had to be somebody else. That thing hanging on the tree had taken away my father, and someone had to pay for that. I didn't care whom.

As the years passed, I felt increasingly guilty at my sin of omission.

We walked down the hill towards the squatters. A thin smoke was coming from black plastic sheets which had been made into a makeshift home around Jacob's Tree. I felt totally unreal, as if in a dream. Other makeshift homes were scattered around, forming a semi-circle around the tree. I heard Tanya taking a short breath and gathering her legal cloak around her. Taking charge, taking control. This was our land. These people had to be evicted.

All of a sudden, she stopped and looked at me, squinting, more like a child than a bigwig lawyer.

'Do we have a plan?' she hissed.

'I thought you had a plan, being a lawyer and all,' I replied in an equally loud whisper.

'Well, I could inform them of the illegality of their action,' she said, in her court voice, sounding totally ridiculous; we were in the bush as far away from any judge, jury or police officer as one could get.

'Okay. Let's just talk to them, then.'

The squatters, twelve of them, had come out of their homes and looked at us. A few registered fear. The rest looked indifferent. We approached, made a greeting and then stood looking at them, somehow inappropriately dressed in our Wallis dresses and £100 Nike shoes.

The leader of the group crawled out of the black plastic shelter and came towards us. After him came an elderly woman. We stood looking at them and they looked back at us. In their rags and coloured traditional cloth, they had more dignity than we did in our foreign clothes.

The leader addressed us. 'So, you have come to kick us out of your land. The land that is dying because nobody is using it. You people surprise me. You want to own land for the sake of owning it. For us, we use land to survive. At least your grandparents took this as their home and lived here. But we do understand. You would rather let the land lie fallow than feed the likes of us.'

Tanya and I looked at each other. We didn't expect this kind of attack. We had expected a group of grovelling, begging villagers. I nudged Tanya to say something, but she seemed frozen.

'Well, the thing is, you are illegally occupying this land which belongs to us. The least you could have done is to let us know, ask for permission, maybe,' I said, hiding behind Tanya.

'Do we look like the kind of people with money for bus fare? Or perhaps madam expected us to walk 200 kilometers to the city to inform her of our illegal action?' the man replied.

We stood there, not knowing what to do. There were twelve of them, eight strong men and three strong women plus the old lady, versus the two of us. I began to see the folly of our behaviour. It would be easy for them to kill us and burn our bodies and nobody would know for quite some time. I think the same thing was going through Tanya's mind.

The old lady whispered something in her son's ear and the man-in-charge turned to us and said, 'My mother says we should all sit down and share some of our home brew while we talk.' Tanya nudged me and the two of us, holding each other's hands, walked towards the shack.

There is nothing like a potent brew of local beer made from the Mapfura fruit to warm the heart and get people talking. We drank more than we should have, but felt too self-conscious to refuse the continuous flow of the beer as the cup was passed around the group.

We talked about the present government, the corruption, and the increasing poverty. Our conversation went back to the past and both of us were shocked to realise that the old lady and her son had lived on the farm, and yet we never saw them. In our childhood, labourers did not exist as individual persons but as a group.

Then, unexpectedly, the old lady said, 'I didn't want us to settle around this tree. I know it is very special for you. Your grandmother gave birth to your father, alone, under this tree. She was very young then, and I understand she had been given in marriage as payment for a debt that her father owed your grandfather's family. I was told this by my own mother.'

Tanya and I sat in total shock. That was the story our grandmother never finished. We were stunned. Our history, given to us while we were in a drunken stupor.

We were dazed, and sat silently as the old woman's voice droned on and on about how her son (Ezekiel, the leader of the settlers) was a good friend of our father from childhood. The son's voice took over and he talked about our father. Ezekial spoke of how our father was like an older brother to him, who had taught him fishing and hunting. Then his face and voice changed and he sounded angry. He stood up and walked away.

We all fell silent. Then the mother said in a tired voice, 'When your father died, they arrested Ezekiel and put him in jail for fifteen years. He was released last year and has not been able to find a job. His father died in shame. He could not understand why Ezekiel would kill Jacob. They were the best of friends from childhood. Like brothers – inseparable.'

I found myself speaking. It was as if the truth was being forced out of me.

'He didn't kill him. I know because I was there.' There was complete and utter silence. Only the sound of non-human creatures could be heard. The chorus of frogs, the mourning of the wind. Ezekiel's voice came up from the darkness.

'I did kill him. It was my fault.'

'No, no, please. I cannot carry this secret anymore.' I cried out. 'My father killed himself. I saw him hanging from the tree. Tanya, I untied the knot and brought him down over there.' Groping in the dust, I used my hands as my eyes in the darkness, pointing to a place which nobody could see.

'No, you don't understand,' Ezekiel said in a tired voice. 'It is true that I didn't hang him. But I hurt him terribly. That day, your father discovered that all your step-siblings are my children. He could not take it, and came here and killed himself. I sensed that he was going to do something drastic. I had taken away his pride. I could have told him that it was all a joke, or I could have followed him and stopped him from hanging himself. But I really wanted to hurt him, so I did kill him due to my act of cruelty.'

A bright moon was slowly rising in the eastern horizon, lighting the faces of the settlers and my sister sitting in a circle in complete silence. Then I heard a sob, terrible in its intensity, and saw Tanya running blindly away from the group. I sat there, feeling lost, not knowing what to do. After a while one of the settlers came and helped me up. I walked slowly with crashing footsteps through the dry grass, getting my dress torn by the fence as I blindly followed my sister to the farm house.

We agreed to let Ezekiel and his family live on the farm and revive it again.

My sister made me promise never to keep secrets from her ever again.

Jacob's Tree still exists. To me, it is a tree of death. To Tanya, it is a tree of life. We don't know what it represents to Ezekiel and his family.

Requiem

Leila Keys

I did not go to Paru's funeral, which appeared to have been a hurried, modest affair. When her sister Shoba telephoned from Bangalore, I was thousands of miles away, back in my home in London. It seemed unreal. I had seen Paru just a week before.

Outside the French windows, snow was falling. It covered the lawn and the roses, soft smooth mounds that made a surreal landscape. Paru had loved the snow. I pictured her in her red snow suit with my two navy-clad boys of seven and five on the snow-covered slopes of Leith Hill in Surrey. I heard her characteristic laughter, mingling with their delighted squeals. It did not seem so very long ago.

More recently, on my visit, I remembered photographs of that tobogganing trip shown proudly to my new husband. ('Your third!' she had said, half-laughing, half-reproachful, 'and I did not manage to have even one!') The photographs were produced to show that she had been beautiful once. But the little boys in the pictures were now grown up, and she herself no longer that vivacious vibrant creature. Moreover, the pictures were silent. They did not convey her laughter, her delightful laughter that started as a chuckle and ended in a squeal, that made people smile to hear it, just the sound of it.

'We dressed her in her favourite orange and gold sari,' Shoba said. 'And she looked lovely.'

No she didn't, I thought dully, with irritation at this feeble attempt to comfort me. Death never allowed anyone to remain lovely, the departing soul leaving no more than a featureless husk behind. But I knew why Shoba had said that. Loveliness had been so important to Paru.

I remembered her buying that orange and gold sari, a wild piece of extravagance to impress a new man in her life. Alas, the man did not last.

'Ah,' she had said later, 'the men go, but the clothes that enchanted them remain to enchant others!'

By then I had come to doubt her nonchalance at the departure of her admirers, and even her pretence that it was always *she* who sent them on their way. That orange sari, however, was special because she was wearing it when she met Duncan, who lasted longer than most, whom she referred to as 'the one'.

The night she met him she could not sleep, and rang to tell me.

'Oh, Paru,' I protested. 'It's three in the morning!'

She was unapologetic. 'I have been up for at least a couple of hours,' she said. 'And do you know what I have been doing?'

'What?' I asked, seduced by the excitement in her voice.

'Painting my picture in my orange sari, and I have got the expression on my face just right. The light over the mirror was fabulous, and the angle of the second mirror perfect. I painted my portrait from my reflection, two reflections, in fact. It is a great picture, Mala, really it is. I can't wait to show you! It absolutely captures this evening which was simply out of this world!'

'Do you remember that self-portrait of hers?' Shoba's voice interrupted, 'and that perfume that she called her signature tune? There was an unopened bottle of that, and we put it in with her, with the portrait. We thought she would be pleased.'

I tried to keep my mind on the conversation, feeling my stomach contract with pain. I wished this conversation would end.

'Tragic,' Shoba said finally. 'Pity she did not have any children!'

I replaced the receiver and looked out at the darkening sky. Paru dead? The meaningless words danced in my head, her lively ebullience making nonsense of the extinction that was death. In the half-light of the silent snow-covered garden, I fancied an orange-clad figure gliding among the dripping apple trees, and thought I could hear the squeal that was her laugh. I had the absurd impulse to open the window and let in a wave of her perfume.

'The most expensive perfume in the world!' she had said, in her usual exaggerated way, when she had discovered it. 'It's what Jackie Kennedy uses. It shall be my signature tune!'

A bright summer afternoon in the garden. She pulls the elegant vial out of her shoulder bag that lies on the grass, takes my hand and sprays my wrist.

'Go on, smell it! Isn't it divine?'

It was. But when she told me what it cost, I nearly fainted.

'At that price, it will be your very own signature tune,' I said. 'There won't be much competition!'

Like that sari, the perfume, with its name 'Joy' by Patou, also became associated with Duncan. 'I didn't think he had seen me, because he didn't once look up,' she said of one of her early tentative encounters with him. 'Later he had said, "Of course I knew you were there. I could smell you! I dared not look up for fear of giving myself away." '

And well he might have been afraid. His wife worked in the casualty department of the same hospital, while he worked with Paru. They were both junior consultant anaesthetists. Their affair was ferociously, flamboyantly passionate. Discretion formed no part of it.

'Oh Paru,' I said in one of my futile remonstrations, 'it is bound to come out, and it will be awful. You will end up losing your job!'

'Since when is it a sacking offence to have an affair? Besides, if anyone gets sacked, why should it be me? I have made no contract to love, honour and cherish! He has!'

'I thought you loved him!'

'Oh, Mala, I do. I do!' Her face was alight with a blissful confidence. 'So when it comes out, there will be an almighty scandal, and he will get chucked out of his cosy marriage, and we will float away into the sunset, or near enough to that, go and live in India. We might even have children. Then I won't have to borrow yours. I'll have my own!'

Four months into the affair, I had a telephone call. It was evening on a Sunday, and the family had gone for a walk. It was autumn, the lawn covered in leaves.

'We haven't met,' a male voice said. 'My name is Duncan. Paru has talked of you a lot.' There was a pause, and I realised the voice was agitated, and I froze with a sense of premonition.

'Is something the matter? With Paru?' I asked fearfully.

'Yes,' he answered. 'I don't know who to call.'

'What is it? Has she had an accident?'

'Yes,' he said again. Then, 'No, not an accident. She has taken a massive overdose. They don't think she will make it!'

When I stood speechless, his voice said into my ear, 'Will you come? At once? Please? She has no one else in this country.'

I sat by Paru as she lay in bed, surrounded by flickering monitors, with tubes and drips, an inert mass. Her eyes were closed.

I tried to pray, but had long since lost the habit, as various gods flitted through my mind, with no one stopping to listen. Irresistibly, the figure of Sister Marie-Thérèse from my convent boarding school came to mind, and I remembered the way we made our deals with God. 'Please, God, I will give up this my most prized possession if you will only . . .'

'What will you give up?' Sister Marie-Thérèse was asking me, and I childishly answered, 'I will never wear Paru's perfume, even if I could buy it!'

The fact that I was giving up something I did not have, and had no real hope of having did not occur to me to be cheating, perhaps because almost all the deals we made in the convent were of this kind, and were no more than a currency of exchange, the language in which we talked to God.

Sister Marie-Thérèse and I were deep in our talk with God when the ward sister appeared and touched me on the arm. I started, and she thought I had been asleep. Perhaps I had been. 'I think you should go and lie down for a bit,' the ward sister was saying. 'You look exhausted!'

It was almost early morning. There seemed little point. I got up obediently. At the end of the corridor, I saw the figure of Duncan, who had been conspicuous by his absence since my arrival. I walked towards him.

'Would you come outside for a minute,' he said. 'I'd like to talk to you.'

We walked out together, down along the corridor into a yard where a path led into the car park. His car, a red sports convertible, stood there in isolation in the early morning light. I remembered with a pang Paru's penchant for sports cars, and for the men who drove them.

'She didn't need to do it,' he said.

He looked at his feet, and clenched his right fist, the left in his jacket pocket. 'She thought she was pregnant, but it turned out that she wasn't.' He lifted both his hands and spread them out, and looked at me in puzzlement. 'There was no need for any of this.'

I know why she thought she was pregnant. Because she forgot that she was ten years older than she had told him she was. She always believed the fantasies she lived by, and she had so longed for children.

I walked back to the ward and sat by her bed, and tried to pray again. But Sister Marie-Thérèse had departed, and I could not re-invoke enough faith even for my ridiculous prayer, a ludicrous attempt to bargain with God. I looked at the inert mass, and wondered what I should do. Tell her family? When, and how much?

Just then, amid the tubes and plaster, something moved on her face. It was no more than a flicker, and I shook my head to rid myself of the illusion. It was no illusion. The eyelids fluttered briefly, and the monitor went wild in tandem with the excitement of the sister, and the staff, who assembled in force.

The scandal was averted. Paru was given sick leave, and came home with me. While in hospital Duncan avoided her, and on the day I went to collect her she tried to see him to say goodbye, while I waited anxiously in the car. He was not available. On the journey home, she cried sporadically, sniffed and dried her eyes and cried again. I made no attempt to comfort her.

That Christmas, a subdued Paru sat in the living room on the blue settee, looking out at the front lawn and the chestnut tree. Night was drawing in, and she was still in her dressing gown. She was monosyllabic, lost in thought. In the next room, the Christmas tree was brilliant with multicoloured lights, and the radio was playing carols. The children had gone carol singing in the neighbourhood. They were a little in awe of this new Paru and kept out of her way.

'Paru,' I said, in desperation. 'You must consider me, just a little. If you just give up like this, what shall I do? Shall I write to your brother?' The despair, the petrified fear in the eyes that turned to mine, stopped me dead. 'Well, obviously, I can't do that,' I added hastily. 'But can't you see I am desperate?'

She made no reply, but got up and went upstairs. In a moment she came down in a bright green caftan, her hair tied back away from her face. In her hand was a gift wrapped in tissue paper, which she first made as if to put under the tree with the other presents. Then she straightened up, and came over and handed it to me.

'I have nothing else,' she said. It was an unopened bottle of Joy.

'I shall never wear it again,' she added sadly.

'Nonsense!' I said briskly. 'We have been here before. Remember your favourite dictum? "Nothing lasts for ever"? Have you forgotten it?'

She didn't answer, and my attempt at humour sounded hollow even to me. She turned and went upstairs.

Christmas came and went, and the old year blended into the new. January was cold, and the London pavements were slippery with frozen snow.

Paru came up to me in the kitchen, an open envelope in her hand. I had cleared away the breakfast things, and was loading the dishwasher. 'I have been offered a job,' she said. 'Locum consultant anaesthetist in Blackburn.' Her face was angry, but her voice was low, expressionless. 'I haven't applied for a job! In Blackburn or anywhere else.'

'I sent off your CV, and signed your name,' I admitted. 'Paru, please don't be angry. You simply must pick up your life again. You know you must.' She stared out of the window in silence. 'Are you angry?'

A blackbird pecked at a crumb. Her voice was forlorn. 'When have I ever been angry with you?'

I put my arm round her, but there was no response to my hug.

Three days later, I was on the platform in Euston, saying goodbye. She looked lost, bemused. I put my hand on hers that lay unresponsive on the open window. 'Paru,' I said. 'Paru, please, please, try!' The train started to move. I took my hand away and blew her a kiss. She raised her hand in a wan gesture, and turned away.

She did not ring to say she had arrived. But when I rang she was unexpectedly reassuring. 'Not bad,' she said, and my heart lifted. 'The people are friendly, and the flat is not bad.' There was a pause, and her voice changed. 'Mala, you gave me back my Christmas present to you. That was not nice. I found it in my shoulder bag when I unpacked.'

'Oh Paru, I didn't mean to give it back, not in the way you think. I just want you to start using it again.'

She changed the subject and asked about the children, and even sounded just a tiny bit animated. I started to have hopes of Blackburn.

I didn't hear from her for a week. When I called, she was usually in the operating theatre. But she always called back, and her voice on the answering machine left busy messages that increasingly reassured me.

Then on a noisy Friday afternoon the telephone rang. It was Paru.

The boys were fighting on the stairs and the TV was adding to the racket. I put my index finger into my ear to shut out the noise, and cupped the receiver tight into my other ear. 'I can't hear you, Paru! What did you say?'

'Stop it!' I shouted at the boys desperately, stamping my foot. Amazingly they stopped, and there was silence.

Paru's voice came over the wire with absolute clarity. 'I took 500 units of insulin last night. By injection. Do you remember our conversations about absolute certainty in suicide? Especially after that botched effort of mine? I am sorry. I wanted to say goodbye.' A petrified pause, and then, 'Goodbye.' The line went dead.

I stood looking at the receiver crouched black and silent on its cradle, and at the boys, their quarrel forgotten, wandering off together into the garden. The hallway and the stairs were eerily still.

I was suddenly seized with panic. I dialled the number of the hospital in Blackburn, and asked to speak to the head of the Anaesthetics Department. I felt lucky as his secretary put me through at once when I said that it was urgent.

He was polite and rather distant as I explained that I was a friend of their new locum anaesthetist, and that I had just had a call to say that she had taken an overdose of insulin the night before.

'Thank you,' he said, after the slightest of pauses and rang off, leaving me unsatisfied and confused.

I rang Paru, and was aware of a distinct disquiet when she answered promptly. I told her I was sorry, but I had rung the head of department. In the silence that followed, I had an overwhelming sense of having done something irretrievably wrong.

'Ah, well,' she said. 'You've just lost me my job. Especially as I didn't go into work today, and called in this morning to say that I had the flu. What would he make of your call telling him that I had taken insulin? That I was not only irresponsible, but a liar as well? Oh, Mala, you did do medicine once, although I do wonder sometimes. Could I have been talking to you this afternoon if I had injected myself with so much insulin last night?'

After that, events blurred into one prolonged nightmare. Paru gave an undertaking that she would not work in the UK, and came to live with me. She cut her hair short, wore miniskirts and giggled a great deal. She thought I was stuffy, prudish and a figure of fun.

One day I wrote to her brother, and he came to England to take her back home to India. Suddenly she was gone. There were a few desultory letters, then silence.

As I sat by the telephone long after Shoba had rung off, it occurred to me that my response to her call had been perfunctory. I looked at the telephone in that darkened room, and again fancied a figure in orange disappearing round the corner of the house. I got up and drew the curtains. 'Tomorrow,' I told myself. 'I'll ring tomorrow.'

A restless night passed in hallucinatory whispers and sudden laughter that had no joy in it. I woke at first light, and came down to find a letter, almost as though it had been left by hand. The postmark said it had been posted a week ago, the day I had left Bangalore after my meeting with Paru. Had the letter been there on the mat the day before? How could I have overlooked it?

Dear Mala,

Fifteen years is a long time. As I stood at the wooden gate of my father's house, watching you drive away with your husband, I felt a familiar loneliness, a sense of *déjà vu*, of being abandoned yet again. The tail lights of the car turned a corner in the lane and disappeared, leaving darkness and silence. I looked back at the house, the windows lit, the light on the porch on, but dim, not really lighting the curved drive to the front steps. I knew there were people in the house, my sister, her family, but I could hear no sound, only this silence that buzzed in my head.

What is it about you that I had longed for but never quite connected with? Whatever it had been, as you drove away with the new man in your life, I knew it had been an illusion, something that had never been there. The realisation brought no relief.

I don't know how long I stood there in the darkness, listening to silence. I am now back in the house, and hear the bustle of children in the main room. Children's voices. They bring a fleeting memory of a forgotten yearning, but it is brief, like a twinge that comes and goes.

Past the empty hall from which the stairs sweep upward to the darkened rooms above, I have come out to the annexe which I call my home, my own little world of sitting room, bedroom and bathroom, with a veranda that leads into the garden, that I have lovingly nurtured in a land of drought and unseasonable downpours. My garden of roses. They are all there; the climbers and the hybrid teas that people bet would never grow in Bangalore. I won every bet.

Just at the moment I cannot see the flowers. I sit instead

in my leather easy chair and look round at my room of books, my collection of music and the large painting of myself on the wall, a painting of me painting myself. There are three reflections in all, each clearer than the next, telling a story that has taken me through many moods. There was a time that the picture brought acute pain, so unbearable that I nearly destroyed that happy expectant face. But the pain and anger went at last, and I grew to love that painting.

This place is mine, I tell myself, as I have done so often in recent years. This place is mine, and in this place I have found peace, forgiven life, forgotten time. This place is mine; mine alone, for here I have at last laid past ghosts to rest.

I thought I had found contentment.

Then came your phone call. 'Where are you?' I asked in sudden confusion as though a voice from the underworld had called.

'Here, two streets away!' Your cheerful voice answered. 'Can I come round?' My heart lifted with a surge of forgotten, explosive delight.

You came round, and sat with me in this room, in this very chair, while I sat on the floor at your feet. The years seemed to roll away, and we were together, laughing, teasing, happy. But soon, with the laughter came the tears, the pain. Then, unbidden, shocking, a word leapt to the forefront of my mind. A word that I had almost kept at bay all these years. Betrayal.

No, not betrayal – betrayals. Yes, there were many betrayals. Betrayals, always dressed up as morally superior decisions made at great cost to you, but which time and again, took their greater toll on me.

You were so good, and I was so bad. You were so pure, and I was always the impure but attractive friend whom you affectionately chastised, and then helpfully rescued from muddles that you had predicted would happen. You always gave, and I took. I never had anything you wanted. Do you remember that bottle of perfume? I thought you liked it. I gave it to you, and of course you returned it, and as always, you had a noble unselfish reason for denying me the role of giver.

I could not stay away from you, and the warmth of your home, and kept finding excuses to come back. You were always kind, but there was always the unspoken feeling of patient righteousness on your part, and importuning unrighteousness on mine.

Then you came up with your final act of betrayal, writing to my brother without telling me. You must have known that there was no turning back then, and I had to come home, to this my family home, a prison that I had left long ago. You told me you had no choice, and I believed that to be true. You told me that it was best for me, and I had to agree.

When you cried at our parting at Heathrow, I cried too, believing as sincerely as you appeared to do, that it was for the best. But best for whom? I have asked myself several times, but the answer was ambiguous until that moment in this room.

We were laughing; recapturing the years we had spent together, back in our early days of easy unquestioning friendship when you said, 'Paru, I have married again!'

As I looked bewildered, you reached for my hand and held it.

'Paru,' you said, 'I am really happy this time. Third time lucky!'

I looked round at my room, remembering my frequent mantra, 'This place is mine. In this place I have found peace and contentment.' The words in my head made no sense.

Then everything changed. Your husband chose to turn up, as though on cue. He was concerned, he said, about how you would get home, and then laughingly added, turning to me, 'I cheated, just a little. I simply had to meet Mala's best friend! She has talked about you so often I feel I know you so well!'

Did he? Know me so well? How could you, or for that matter he, know me, when I hardly knew you, or myself, until I found this place, my place, from where I looked back at life and understood so much? The rest of the evening was a blur, until I stood at the gate watching you drive away.

Now I am back here, with the darkened garden that I can no longer see, the roses there the replica of the roses in your home. I look at the picture on the wall and it looks back at me with a witch's grimace. It is suddenly frightening to look at.

This place is no longer mine, and I am a stranger. You have expropriated it as you have done the rest of my life.

Fifteen years. It took me fifteen years to find a place that I thought was my own, only to find that that is an illusion too.

There the letter ended.

There was no signature. I picked up the envelope, and looked once again at the postmark. The day after our visit.

I telephoned Shoba.

'Shoba,' I said without preamble. 'We have known each other for years. So tell me. Did Paru kill herself?'

There was a pause, and the expected answer came.

'Yes,' she said.

About the Authors

Jo Campbell began writing about three years ago, following retirement from the Civil Service. 'Yanks' is her first published story. She lives with her husband in North London and belongs to a writing class.

Tania Casselle is a freelance magazine writer. She was a finalist in the Raymond Carver Short Story Award and has also published poetry in literary magazines and anthologies. She is currently working on a novel. She lives in London.

Frances Childs was born in London in 1971. She started writing three years ago and her first two plays, *The Light Fingered Philosopher* and *Peacehaven Ward*, were performed on the London Fringe and in Brighton. Frances tours the country as an actor and puppeteer with *Bodger and Badger Live*, the children's show. She is working on her first novel, *Beautiful Symmetry*. She lives in Brighton.

Fiona Curnow has had over 100 short stories published in the UK and US. She also writes poetry and is the poetry editor for *Cadenza* magazine. Her fiction encompasses literary, commercial and women's erotica. Her first novel, under her erotica pen name, Maria Lyonesse, is published by X Libris under the title *Lust Under Leo*. She has two small daughters, lives in Worcestershire and enjoys folk festivals, red wine and chocolate.

Louise Doughty has published three novels – *Crazy Paving*, *Dance With Me* and *Honey-Dew*. She has also written three plays for radio and is well known as an arts critic and cultural commentator for press, radio and TV.

Patricia Duncker is Reader in English at the University of Wales, Aberystwyth, where she teaches writing, and nineteenth- and twentieth-century literature. She is the author of *Hallucinating Foucault*, *Monsieur Shoushana's Lemon Trees*, and *James Miranda Barry*, all published by Serpent's Tail. Her most recent publications are *The Deadly Space Between* and a collection of essays, *Writing on the Wall*.

Magi Gibson's second collection of poetry, *Wild Women of a Certain Age*, is published by Chapman of Edinburgh. Her poetry appears regularly in Scottish literary magazines.

A. L. Kennedy is author of two prize-winning collections of short stories, three award-winning novels and *Original Bliss*: short stories and a novella. She has also written two non-fiction books and a variety of journalism. She has been a Booker Prize judge, has written for the stage, film and TV and has edited various anthologies and publications. She was listed among Granta's best of Young British novelists. She is a Fellow of both the Royal Society of Literature and the Royal Society of Arts and has sold brushes door-to-door.

Leila Keys has had a short story published in the Asham Award anthology, the *The Catch*, and her short stories have been broadcast on BBC Radio Four. She is now working on a novel. She was born in India and is a practising psychiatrist in London.

Elena Lappin is a novelist and journalist living in London. She is the author of a book of short stories, *Foreign Brides*, and a novel, *The Nose*, both published by Picador. She is currently working on her next collection of stories.

Linda Leatherbarrow won the Bridport Prize in 2001 and has been three times winner of the London Writers' Competition. Her stories have been published in various anthologies and magazines and have been broadcast on BBC Radio Four. In 1995 she set up the Haringey Literature Festival and coordinated it for three years. She teaches at Middlesex University and the City University, London.

Rowena Macdonald was born on the Isle of Wight in 1974. She grew up in the West Midlands before moving to Brighton to study English at Sussex University. After a stint as a reporter on the *Sussex Express*, she spent a year in Montreal writing her first novel and working as a waitress. She now lives in London, works at the House of Commons and is writing her second novel.

Ravai Marindo was born in Masvingo, in rural Zimbabwe. Having recently returned from living in Britain, she now resides in Harare. Apart from fiction writing, her interests include reproductive health research, gardening, hiking and mbira playing.

Jenny Mitchell is a fulltime writer whose work has appeared in the *Guardian*, *Observer* and *Pride Maga-*

zine. In 2000 she was made Poet-in-Residence of the Westway in Ladbroke Grove; and in 2001 she was nominated as Best Writer New to Radio for her play *English Rose* (Radio Four). Her work has been dramatised on BBC television (*The English File*), and her poems have appeared in several anthologies. 'The Master and the Maid' is part of a collection called *Full Freedom*.

Georgia Moseley gained a distinction for her Masters in History which she completed at the University of Sussex in September 2001. She now lives in London and works for the BBC as a production trainee.

Kate Pullinger is a Canadian writer based in London. Her books include the novels *The Last Time I Saw Jane*, *Where Does Kissing End?* and, most recently, *Weird Sister*, as well as the short story collection, *My Life as a Girl in a Men's Prison*. Kate Pullinger also writes for film; she co-wrote the novel of the film *The Piano* with Jane Campion. She has lectured and taught widely; in 1995/96 she was Judith E. Wilson Visiting Fellow at Jesus College, Cambridge and in 2001/02 was visiting Writing Fellow at the Women's Library at London Guildhall University. She teaches online at the trAce Writing School and is Research Fellow at trAce, looking at new forms of online narrative and new media writing.

Carol Shields has published many novels and two collections of short stories. *The Stone Diaries* was shortlisted for the Booker Prize and won the Pulitzer Prize for Fiction in 1995. She won the Orange Prize with *Larry's Party* in 1998. Her collection of short fiction *Dressing Up for the Carnival* was published in 2000. Her latest novel, *Unless*, published in 2002, has inspired the short story 'Here's' which appears in this anthology. She lives in Victoria, British Columbia.

Ling E. Teo spent the first nineteen years of her life in Singapore and the following nine in the UK. She now lives, paints, and writes in Portland, Oregon.